Assault on Fort Bennett

It is 1866 and Colonel Thomas Sykes, late of the Confederate Army, is in Milledgeville gaol, waiting to be hanged, but he is pardoned and freed from prison, on condition that he helps find and release the president's niece, who is being held by a band of comancheros.

This task proves to be far from straightforward and the colonel finds himself out of his depth when he is called upon to help assemble a number of Gatling guns which have been stolen from the army. Colonel Sykes will soon find himself caught in the middle of a fierce battle between the comancheros on the one hand and a troop of US Cavalry on the other. Will he succeed in his mission?

By the same author

Whirlwind

Assault on Fort Bennett

Fenton Sadler

A Black Horse Western

ROBERT HALE · LONDON

ISBN 978-0-7198-1364-1

Robert Hale Limited
Clerkenwell House
Clerkenwell Green
London EC1R 0HT

www.halebooks.com

Typeset by
Derek Doyle & Associates, Shaw Heath
Printed and bound in Great Britain by
CPI Antony Rowe, Chippenham and Eastbourne

CHAPTER 1

The noise of the hammering and sawing woke Sykes early that morning. He yawned and stretched before getting out of bed and peering through the barred window. His cell was on the top floor of the penitentiary and so he could see across the wall surrounding the exercise yard and into the town itself. The stark wooden framework of the gallows upon which he and three other men were to hang the next day was clearly visible. After executions the structure would be dismantled and stored in an old coach-house until the next time that it was needed. Because erecting it was a tiresome job, which always entailed some repairs and minor adjustments, the custom was to wait until there were at least three or four condemned men and then hang them all in one go.

From a cell along the corridor somebody called out, 'Hey, Colonel, you ready for your big day?'

'I am vastly obliged to you,' Sykes called back. 'Yes, I think that I shall be ready in time for the performance tomorrow morning. At least I know that the show cannot begin until I have arrived.' The men in the cells along the corridor laughed and told each other that Colonel Sykes surely had a right dry sense of humour.

There was a boisterous, if grim, camaraderie among the inmates of the prison. There was also a strict hierarchy, with common thieves at the bottom and decent murderers like Sykes at the top. The fact that he had until last year been a full colonel in the Confederate Army gave Sykes added prestige, as did the nature of his crime. That he was also due to be executed the next day meant that, all things considered, Colonel Thomas Sykes was right at the top of the jail's pecking order. His casual and good-humoured acceptance of the fate that awaited him also endeared him greatly to the other prisoners.

From the next cell Sykes could hear a whimpering sound, which put him in mind of a dog that has been whipped. The terrified moaning and snivelling was being made by a fellow prisoner called Barkis, who had been sentenced to death for poisoning his own child for the insurance money; a hideous crime, even by the standards prevailing in the prison. Colonel Sykes called out to the man.

'Brace up, for the Lord's sake, Barkis. Be a man. We all have to die one day, you know.'

His words had the opposite effect to that which he had intended, because on hearing the word 'die', the frightened man cried out, 'Oh, God!' and redoubled his lamentations. Sykes decided that there was little point in saying anything more to such a person.

Shortly after breakfast had been served, a meal consisting of a bowl of thin gruel washed down by a small mug of watery coffee with a distinctly tinny taste, Colonel Sykes's cell door was unlocked and a warder told him that he was wanted in the governor's office. This was unusual and Sykes wondered what it might portend. He soon found out.

There were two other men with the governor in his office. One was a uniformed soldier: a captain in the cavalry. The other was a natty-looking civilian, expensively dressed and with the air of importance that comes from working close to the government. Probably, thought the colonel, a senior civil servant from Washington.

'Well, Sykes,' began the governor, 'I hope that you are prepared to die in the morning?'

'My dear sir,' replied the colonel politely, 'if you have invited me here to offer spiritual consolation, then I really must protest. That is the proper business of the chaplain. What will you be asking next: whether or not I am immortally saved?'

'None of this has any reference to the next life, Colonel Sykes,' said the man in civilian clothes. 'We are rather offering you the opportunity to extend your stay in this world. I have here a pardon, signed by President Johnson himself. It relieves you from the painful necessity of being hanged tomorrow morning.' He handed the document to Colonel Sykes, who read it with an unusual amount of interest, tending as it did towards the important matter of his own life or death.

Dated and signed by the President on 22 April 1866, the sheet of paper in his hands remitted all punishment due to Colonel Thomas Abernethy Sykes for the crime of murder, of which he had been convicted the previous month. The messenger who had brought this pardon to Milledgeville must have been in a rare hurry to travel through the night so that he might deliver it here by nine in the morning. This in turn suggested to the colonel that the matter was mighty important to somebody.

Sykes handed the pardon back to the man and said, 'If this is part of some bargain, whereby I am expected to betray the cause for which I fought, then you may take it away again. I will have no part of it.'

The other three men in the room could not help but admire such a principled stand. Here was a man due to suffer a degrading death within twenty-four hours and yet he could cheerfully consider rejecting the means of saving his own life.

The cavalry officer spoke. 'With your permission, gentlemen, perhaps I can make matters a little clearer to the colonel? Colonel Sykes, my name is Stanton, Captain James Stanton. Nobody is asking you to betray anybody. We are trying rather to save the life of an unfortunate young woman. As you perhaps know, we are having a great deal of trouble with the Comanche and Kiowa in Texas and New Mexico. They are being aided by the comancheros down that way and short of launching a full-scale war, there is little that we are able to do to bring the area under control.'

'All this is tolerably well known to me,' said Colonel Sykes. 'My own war ended, though, with the surrender at Appomattox last year. Why are you telling me all this?'

'A month ago,' continued the cavalry officer, 'a stagecoach was intercepted, either by Indians or comancheros, we don't rightly know which. Some of the male passengers were killed, but a girl of twenty has been missing ever since. We have received reports that she is still alive.'

'Once again,' said the colonel, 'all very interesting. Where do I come into the picture?'

The well-dressed man who had handed Sykes the presidential pardon cut in at this point. 'Here is the full situation, Colonel. The young woman who was taken from that stage is President Johnson's niece. She is the only kin remaining to him. It is his personal wish that every effort be made to rescue this girl. We know that you commanded forces in New Mexico during the late war and that you speak fluent Spanish. It is also known that if anybody would be trusted by these rogues, it is a man such as yourself who fought fiercely against the Federal army. We want you to find this girl and bring her to safety.'

'I shall need time to consider such a proposition,' said Sykes coolly. 'May I give you my answer this afternoon?'

'You may not,' said the civilian. 'Do not try and fox with us in this way, Colonel. It will not answer here. Will you save your life by undertaking this task?'

'Am I to work alone to this end?'

'There would be little point otherwise,' said the captain. 'I don't think that you would do very well over in New Mexico if you were to be accompanied by a troop of US Cavalry. If that would do the trick, then we should hardly have to come here, cap in hand, asking for your help. What we ask from you is a pledge that you will do all in your power to free this girl from her captors and look after her until she is in a place of safety.'

'What is to hinder my running off, once I am freed?'

'Nothing,' said the civilian. 'Nothing except your honour. If you agree to this, then we shall require a promise from you. I know that you have never yet broken your oath; I doubt that you would start now.'

The colonel hooked his thumbs in his belt and beat a little tattoo with his fingers upon the leather, a trick of his when thinking hard. At length he announced, 'Very well then. If you will all offer me your solemn assurance that you are not asking me to play the part of a spy or betray such of my former comrades as I might come across during this enterprise, and that the sole, immediate and direct object is the freeing of a young woman from captivity, then I accept.'

After being escorted back to his cell, while the various arrangements were made for his release, Sykes lay on the bunk and considered whether he had done the right thing in taking up this offer. Of course, it went without saying that he had no more wish than the next man to be hanged by the neck.

10

There were, though, more important things in this world than death and the colonel had always lived his life according to his own rigid code of honour. He would have scorned to ransom his life by a lie or other dishonourable act. From what he could see of the game, though, certainly as represented by those men in the governor's office, that was very far from being the case here. He would be saving a young woman from a bunch of cut-throats and brigands and he was to be rewarded with his freedom. It looked to him to be a true bill.

Plainly, those who had offered him this deal did not altogether trust him. He had been told that it would be necessary for him to remain in his cell until the next day. This was irksome, but quite under-standable. Using presidential power in this way for a personal end was not something that anybody in Washington would wish to see noised abroad, and the safest way of maintaining a certain level of secrecy was to keep Sykes locked up until the time came for him to leave Milledgeville and head west.

It would, thought Colonel Sykes to himself, be mere affectation to pretend that he was not delighted to find that he was after all to live beyond the next day. No man is indifferent to his own death. Even so, he wondered what this business would mean to him. But there, it surely would be pleasant to be a free man again, with a gun in his hand and a mission to perform. Fighting had been his life for so long that, since the end of the War between the States, he had begun to find the peace wearisome and the days

11

dragging. A little excitement would not come at all amiss.

Prisons are seldom restful places and the nights before executions are often marked by disturbance of one sort or another. Sykes was woken at dawn by screams and cries from the cell next to his. He lay there for a time and gradually realized that the sounds were caused by warders trying to get Barkis dressed. From all that he was able to collect, the man was in an absolute paroxysm of fear and despair and resisting all attempts to get him into his clothes.

The executions were scheduled to be conducted at ten that morning. Sykes wondered if the warders had been briefed at the change of plan regarding his own part in the drama. How ironic if nobody had remembered to tell them and they took him out and hanged him anyway! He need not have worried. A little after half-past nine he was once again taken to the governor's office. This time only the governor and the cavalry officer were waiting for him.

The captain asked Colonel Sykes if he was ready to leave. He replied that he was and then addressed the governor, saying, 'I cannot leave this place without observing that you, sir, are a damned rascal. I have had ample evidence of your thievery, such as the inadequate food that you supply to the men in your charge while doubtless pocketing much of the money you are paid for feeding the prisoners here. You also take bribes from factories and mills for allowing them to lease out your convicts under conditions which are worse than slavery. I hope, sir, that

12

your crimes will ultimately catch up with you and that
you will yourself end by being imprisoned in this very
jail.'

The governor first went white and then scarlet.
After that his face became suffused with purple, as he
began spluttering an indignant denial of these
charges. Ignoring him utterly, the colonel said to the
cavalry officer, 'Perhaps you would now be kind
enough to conduct me from this pest-hole, Captain?'

An immense throng of people packed the square
in front of the gallows. So focused was the attention
of the crowd upon the four nooses hanging from the
forbidding wooden structure that nobody took any
notice of the two riders who had paused on the out-
skirts of the mass of spectators.

'Somebody forgot to tell the hangman,' observed
the colonel.

'How's that?' asked the blue-coated cavalryman at
his side.

'I was to hang with three others. There are still
four nooses.'

'Oh yes, I see what you mean.'

They sat there, unable to draw themselves away
from the dreadful event unfolding in front of them.
Two of those being executed that morning walked up
the steps to the platform without any assistance. The
third man, however, had to be dragged up, screaming and struggling. It was Barkis. The chaplain led
the crowd in a prayer and then suggested that they
sing a hymn together. While those with their feet on
solid ground sang 'Amazing Grace', the men waiting

to be hanged just stood there, as though uncertain of what to do next. Leastways, two of them did; Barkis was still trying to break free of those holding his arms.

When the hymn was over the three condemned men were guided to their places and their feet strapped together. They were then hooded and noosed. A second later the trapdoors fell with an echoing boom as the men were launched into eternity. Colonel Sykes could not help rubbing his throat thoughtfully and meditating upon what so very nearly had come to pass for him.

'Close shave,' said Captain Stanton.

'You might well say so,' replied Sykes. 'Tell me, how are we to reach New Mexico?'

'We will ride to Macon, get the railroad north and then change on to the Atchison, Topeka and Kansas line.'

'And do you mean to accompany me every step of the way?'

'Those are my instructions, yes.'

It was a beautiful sunny spring morning and Colonel Sykes could think of many worse ways to spend a few hours than riding through the open countryside between Macon and Milledgeville. The cavalry officer seemed to be a decent enough fellow, for a Yankee, and they chatted about this and that as they travelled. One thing that had been bothering Sykes was that he had no change of clothes, nor any of his guns.

The captain said, 'You need not make yourself uneasy about that. One of my men visited your home yesterday evening and packed a trunk for you. It should arrive at the station in Macon ahead of us.'

'You make very free with my belongings,' said Colonel Sykes.

'As I see it, sir, you are alive and have no cause for complaint.'

As they talked the two men discovered that they had both been at some of the same engagements during the war, although naturally on opposite sides. The conversation turned after a time to the subject of Sykes's late imprisonment.

Captain Stanton said, 'Tell me, why were you about to be hanged? I know only that you were convicted of murder and that you killed a soldier.'

'May I speak to you as man to man? That is to say, you will not report what I tell you to your superiors or relay it to anybody else?'

'That goes without saying,' said the captain a little stiffly. 'We are both officers.'

'I meant no offence,' said Colonel Sykes. 'This is the way of it. One of those soldiers from your army occupying Milledgeville committed an unspeakable crime upon a young girl. He was arrested by the provost guard and would have faced trial. The wretch disputed the matter and made an infamous claim about the girl, that she was a willing participant to his beastly act. She would have had to give evidence in court, with everybody knowing her shame. Her father would have killed her first before he allowed

15

that to happen. So I and one or two others called on the fellow, who had been freed on bail. We gave him the chance to take his own life, which he refused. So we hanged him.'

Stanton said nothing for a while, then asked, 'Would you have done the same had he not been a soldier from the North?'

'I would have done the same had he been my own brother,' said Colonel Sykes grimly.

The ride to Macon passed pleasantly enough and that evening the two men settled down into a train heading north. The colonel's trunk had arrived at the station before them and their horses were left at livery in Macon. Captain Stanton assured Sykes that he would be able to provide him with the very best in horseflesh when they reached New Mexico.

Once the train was fairly on its way Colonel Sykes said to Stanton, 'Captain, if I am to find this young person and free her, then I need to know somewhat about the situation with the comancheros.'

'That's no great mystery,' said the other. 'As perhaps you know, they trade with the Comanche and Kiowa. Attempts are being made to get those Indians on to reservations and the comancheros don't like it. It would deprive them of their livelihood. Lately they have been running guns to the Comanche and generally making a nuisance of themselves.'

'Why have they taken this girl? Do they know that she is related to the President?'

'Hard to say,' said Captain Stanton. 'At a guess,

16

probably not. They do take young women from time to time. Some are ransomed; that is to say they are, in effect, sold back to their families. There has been no communication from the comancheros about this girl, so we guess that they don't know who she is. Other young women are sometimes sold south of the border to Mexican brothels. Whether this fate has befallen Elizabeth Harper, that is to say the girl in question, we simply don't know.'

'Just to be sure that we understand each other, Captain, I will only operate alone. It would compromise me fatally if anybody were to suspect that I am working hand in glove with the army on this matter.'

'That is perfectly understood, sir. We will travel together to a base some good way from where the girl was seized. You can have your pick of horses and also any equipment you might require. After that, you will be on your own.'

Colonel Sykes looked out of the window, his eyes scanning the distant horizon. 'This,' he said, 'promises to be a right entertaining little adventure.'

CHAPTER 2

By an unfortunate coincidence Colonel Sykes's thirty-seventh birthday chanced to fall on the very day that he was sentenced to death. For his part, he found the combination of circumstances grotesque and not a little amusing. In the morning he had received best wishes for a long and prosperous life from the various friends and family members who were permitted to visit him in jail and that same afternoon he was condemned to hang by the neck until he was dead. You would, thought Sykes at the time, need to be utterly devoid of any sense of the ridiculous not to see the funny side of this sequence of events.

When the war started with the shelling of Fort Sumter in 1861, Thomas Sykes had already been in the army for fourteen years, having been a West Point cadet since leaving school. He began the war as a captain and finished as a colonel. The army was all that he had known for the whole of his adult life, and the peace had left him bereft, as though he had lost a family. As a high-ranking officer he was not eligible to take the Ironclad Oath and so he retired to the farm that his father had left him. It was overgrown and neglected, having been maintained before the war by slaves. Sykes could not afford to pay for freed workers and had somehow struggled on, working the land by himself.

His fame as a soldier was great, and when the rigours of military occupation by the Federal forces became ever harsher he was approached by some former members of the Confederate Army and asked if he wished to join a movement pledged to resist the occupation. He had declined. The rumours reaching him about the activities of the Ku Klux Klan did not incline him favourably towards membership of that organization.

The hanging of the Yankee soldier for the rape of a sixteen-year-old girl, in which he had assisted, did not seem to Colonel Sykes to be a crime: more a matter of common justice. He had not been overly surprised to be arrested and sent for trial, nor unduly shocked when sentence of death was pronounced. His fellows in the enterprise had managed to escape to Texas a couple of steps ahead of the military patrol sent to detain them.

Which brought Sykes to this present pass: bound for the area where he had spent part of the war. A better man for this job could hardly have been found. Although his father had been American, his mother was Spanish. She had been so dark that her son was sometimes mistaken for a mulatto. From her, he had learned as a child to speak Spanish as fluently as he did English. Since the comancheros themselves were of Spanish–Mexican stock, a command of the language would be invaluable if he wished to get close enough to them to find what had become of the missing girl.

Night came and both Colonel Sykes and the young cavalry officer sitting opposite him fell asleep, dozing fitfully until the morning.

By the time that they reached Albuquerque Colonel Sykes and Captain Stanton had probably had about enough of each other's company to last a good long while. When all was said and done they were no more than chance companions thrown together by circumstance and, despite making the best of it, they were neither of them keen to prolong the acquaintance. Nevertheless, they had little choice, because the captain had still to deliver Sykes to the army base at Edgewood.

A carriage was waiting for them when they left the station at Albuquerque. The colonel's trunk was loaded on to it and the two men climbed in.

'Now that we are a little closer to the scene,' said Stanton, 'I feel that I should give you some more information on this affair.'

'Yes, I had you pegged for a man who played his cards close to his chest,' said Colonel Sykes. 'I thought that there was more to the case than you had so far told me.'

'You likely know that there is now an Austrian in

charge in Mexico and that he is backed by French troops?'

'I had heard of this, yes. He arrived in the same year that the war started.'

'Well,' said Captain Stanton, 'not to put too fine a point on it, we want the French out of the country. We've had a mite too much of the Europeans interfering on this continent. There are men in Mexico who wish to see an end to this famous emperor of theirs.'

'Meaning, I suppose, that you are supplying these rebels with arms. I can see that doing this, while at the same time fighting the Comanche and Kiowa and trying to drive them from their land, is stretching your army's resources to their limit.'

'Meaning,' said Stanton, more than a little nettled, 'that the Mexican border is so tense that we do not wish to start a war by sending an army to hunt for the President's niece. Not to mention that anybody holding her would probably just kill her out of hand and bury the body, if once they thought that the army were on their tail. Which is, of course, where you come into the picture.'

Edgewood Camp had, to Colonel Sykes's practised eye, the appearance of an army base at time of war. Several hundred troops were stationed here and loaded wagons were arriving and departing in a more or less continuous stream. Sykes guessed that this was a staging post, where troops and arms first arrived from the north and were then relayed to the Mexican border. It was rash in the extreme of those running such a clandestine operation to allow a former officer of the Confederate Army to sniff around, and this served only to reinforce his view that President Johnson was absolutely desperate to regain his relative. The story was that he was a lonely man who had fallen out with all his family years previously. Perhaps this was his way of making amends.

Major Sterne, the commander of Edgewood, was not exactly effusive in his welcome.

'I have been instructed to offer you every facility, Colonel Sykes,' he said. 'Although, as God knows, I think you would have been better hanged for that brutal murder. Still, I was not consulted. My adjutant will show you round and you are to choose a horse and whatever you might need in the way of arms and equipment.'

'I am obliged to you,' said the colonel politely. 'I have a trunk with me. I may, I suppose, leave that here and also be given a room in which to tidy up a little and prepare myself?'

'Leave your trunk here?' said Major Sterne irritably. 'What do you suppose I am running, a left-luggage office?'

'Have you not been instructed to offer me every assistance? That, at least, was my understanding.'

'The Lord only knows why they have asked a rogue like you to help out in whatever matter this concerns. I suppose it was because you rode with that scoundrel Sibley, when he invaded this territory and looted and burned his way through it.'

'I had the honour to serve under General Sibley, if that is what you mean. And we whipped you men until you ran for your very lives, or had you forgot?'

'Not for long you didn't, Sykes. Or have *you* forgotten how your little adventure ended? When we counter-attacked and chased you boys right back to San Antonio.'

'This is all very interesting, Major Sterne, but I'm sure that President Johnson did not engage me to bandy words with you in this fashion.'

After a little more ill-natured banter of this sort, Sykes was given a room for the day and took his leave of Captain Stanton. Then Sterne's adjutant showed the colonel round the base and allowed him to select what he thought he might need for the job in hand. When he had chosen a horse and also collected various useful items from the stores, Sykes asked to be left alone for a space to shave and change.

Now, Colonel Sykes had not thought it necessary to be altogether open and honest with those who had asked him to undertake this mission. For instance, he had not mentioned that he had in the past had dealings with a number of bands of comancheros and could make an educated guess as to where this girl was being held; assuming, that was, that she was still alive and a prisoner of the comancheros and not of their Kiowa or Comanche allies.

The dangerous part would be persuading the comancheros that he was sympathetic to their cause and not meaning harm to them. Actually, as far as it went, this was true. Sykes could not for the life of him see why the Northern Army could not just leave these people in peace and stop harrying them around the territory. He was astonished at the hypocrisy of these Northerners, who one minute were wringing their hands over the plight of black men in the South and the next were hunting down and slaughtering the Indians as though they were vermin. Still, that was nothing to the purpose. His only aim was to free that one young woman.

There was a knock at the door. When he opened it, there stood the adjutant.

'Major Sterne's compliments, sir, and he wonders if you could spare him a few minutes?'

Once the two of them were alone in his office, Sterne said, 'I have not been told what you are doing or why. That is just fine by me.' He handed Colonel Sykes an envelope. 'I was told to give you this when you were ready to leave. I want you to sign for the equipment that you are taking with you. We shall expect it back again.'

Sykes read through the list which the major gave him. It said:

1 0.58 Springfield's Rifle Musket
1 0.44 Colt Army revolver
1 5 lb keg of fine-grain black powder
1 Box copper percussion caps
1 20 ft length of fuse
1 Pair of field glasses

Once he had signed the list the colonel said, 'You might not get back all the powder, you know. I may need to do some shooting.'

'Just bring back what you are able,' said Major Sterne shortly.

'You will permit me to observe, Major, that it has been anything but a pleasure dealing with you,' said Sykes amiably. 'I only wish that we had met a year or two back, at a time when we could have exchanged shots with each other rather than words.'

It was childish of him, but Colonel Sykes found that he was gaining a great deal of amusement from bating the Union officer, who, under the circumstances, could do little other than grit his teeth and endure Sykes's taunts. The two men did not part on good terms.

Half an hour after leaving the base at Edgewood, Colonel Sykes reined in his horse and simply revelled in the feeling of being a free man with a useful task in hand. He had been adrift since the end of the war. Having been a colonel in the Confederate army meant that his military career was now over, and he had been no great shakes as a farmer. Now he was armed to the teeth and if not actually a soldier once more, he was at least undertaking a soldier's job.

The envelope that the commandant had given him contained nothing of any use. It merely gave the location of the stagecoach when it had been ambushed and the names of some of the better-known leaders of groups of comancheros. None of that would help. Sykes had headed south from Edgewood until he was out of sight and then changed tack and worked his way round until he was going north-east. There was no percentage in letting anybody at the army base know where he was heading. All those who had been dealing with this problem had assumed that if the girl was still alive then she would be with a bunch of men near the Mexican border. This did not strike Colonel Sykes as at all likely. The real strongholds of the comancheros were to be found not on the border, but up on the high plains nearer to Colorado.

Unless things had changed dramatically in the last year or two there were only two places where captives could be held securely for any length of time. One of these was Palo Duro canyon over in Texas and the other was the area known as Cejita de los Comancheros. This consisted of hundreds of square miles of the high plains. Nobody lived around there other than the Indians and comancheros and even the army did not trouble them.

As he headed east Sykes recalled vividly the last time that he had been in this area. It had been four years ago, almost to the day, and he had been riding along this very track towards Cejita de los Comancheros. At that time, of course, in the spring of 1862, he had not been alone. He had been one of thousands of retreating Confederate soldiers: men who had been part of a bold and daring attempt to win the War between the States by an unexpected thrust west.

26

After a year of war the fighting between the Union and the Confederacy was in the main restricted to the border between the two powers. Most of the action, the actual fighting, was around Virginia. Elsewhere, it had relapsed into somewhat of a stalemate, resembling in some degree medieval siege warfare, with both sides dug in along fortified lines. General Sibley had approached President Davis with an audacious plan. What if an army were to be dispatched from Texas and sent west through New Mexico? Might it not be possible to seize both the Colorado goldfields and the Pacific ports of California? This would have the effect both of depriving the Union of large monetary reserves and of relieving their naval blockade of the Confederacy.

It was while musing upon those lost glories that the colonel gradually became aware of cries of distress; a woman was in difficulties, unless he was very much mistaken. The sounds were coming from the other side of a heap of boulders which lay to one side of the track. Sykes guided his horse in that direction and rode round the little mound. The scene which met his eyes roused him in a moment to hot fury. Three figures were struggling in the dust. Two of the people scuffling were white men, the third an Indian woman. The men were holding the woman down and simultaneously attempting to force themselves upon her, while a third man, little more than a boy by the look of him, stood irresolutely to one side.

'What's the case?' said Colonel Sykes in an authoritative and commanding voice. 'What are you men about with that woman?'

One of the men who had been struggling with the Indian woman let go and left his partner to try and restrain her by himself. He walked a little way towards the colonel and said sharply, 'What's it to you? You looking for a fight?'

'I'm not looking for anything much,' said Sykes mildly. 'I have business of my own. But I'm damned if I'll see a woman mistreated. You men leave her be now, or we are likely to fall out.'

The man to whom he was speaking looked positively villainous to Sykes. He was a tall, gangling fellow of about thirty, with a mean and cunning look about him. His appearance was not improved by a long, crooked scar which covered one side of his face in an irregular pink seam. He was evidently not a man used to having his passions thwarted because, with no further words, his hand snaked down to the pistol at his hip. Sykes had an advantage, because it was a peculiarity of his never to use a holster. He had the Colt Army tucked into his belt and because he was riding, his hand was naturally only a few inches from the grip of his weapon. He had drawn and shot the man down before the other had even touched his own piece.

The two other men seemed to be thoroughly taken aback by this turn of events. The younger one, who had not been taking an active part in the assault on the woman, made a swift and sensible decision, throwing up his hands at once. The one who still had a hold of the Indian could not apparently decide whether to release her and shoot at the man on horseback or to continue with whatever plans he had for the woman.

The decision was taken out of his hands, because the woman managed to get a hand free. She raked her nails down his cheek, causing him to let go of her. He pushed her violently to one side and then went for his gun.

Sykes did not wish to kill anybody else needlessly and had already drawn down on the fellow as soon as he was apart from the woman. This gave him time to aim carefully and his ball took the man in the wrist rather than his chest. The pistol the man had pulled fell from his hand and he screamed in pain.

Colonel Sykes turned quickly to see if the youngest of the three men posed any kind of threat, but the boy was still standing with his hands raised above his head.

'Don't shoot me, mister,' he said. 'I had no part of this.'

'Are those men I shot friends of yours?'

'Not hardly. I only met them yesterday. I swear I didn't know what they purposed when they grabbed the squaw.'

Colonel Sykes thought it over for a second and then said, 'You're full young, which I will allow as an extenuating circumstance. But I tell you plain, I cannot abide such goings on as this. You be on your way now. You hear what I tell you?'

As the young man lowered his hands and turned

to leave, relieved that this grim-faced stranger was apparently not going to kill him, there came a blood-curdling scream. Sykes, who had a good deal of experience of the various noises made by men in extreme agony, had never heard anything like it in the whole course of his life. He turned at once to the source of the inhuman shrieking, just a fraction of a second too late to prevent the Indian woman's final bloody vengeance for the indignity to which she had been subjected.

From somewhere – Sykes found afterwards that it had been in the belt of the man he had shot dead – the woman had obtained a Bowie knife. The fellow whom he had only winged had sunk to his knees and was nursing his shattered wrist, which must have been exquisitely painful. While his attention had been fully occupied in holding his arm still and trying to assess the extent of the damage, the Indian woman had taken the knife from the dead man, gone up to the one who was only wounded and stabbed him twice: once in each eye. Mercifully, his suffering was not prolonged, because she followed up by plunging the blade through his throat, causing him to choke rapidly to death on his own blood.

The boy stared in horror, saying in a strangled and barely audible tone, 'God almighty, she juked out his eyes.'

'Well,' said Sykes, 'that's the sort of thing that happens when you start down the road of assaulting women and trying to take advantage of them. Those men had it coming.' All of which Sykes felt to be quite true, but even so he was shocked at the ferocity with which the young woman had exacted her revenge. He said, 'Go along now, son, and let that be a warning to you.'

As the young man went over to his horse and mounted up Sykes went to the woman and said, 'Well, missy, I reckon you have paid him back now. Just hand me that knife, will you?' He held out his hand and whether or not she understood the words, she recognized the gesture and handed him the weapon. 'Do you speak much English?' he asked.

'A little, little,' replied the woman, who could not have been more than eighteen or twenty.

'I had best take you to your kin,' said Colonel Sykes. 'Notwithstanding the fact that I am in the deuce of a hurry. Do you live near here?'

'Visit family,' said the girl, pointing east. 'Live there.'

'Well then, it seems our paths lie alongside for a spell.'

The Indian woman had a tough little piebald pony, which she rode well. She and Sykes trotted along the track, neither speaking, and the colonel began to wonder how he would be able to rid himself of this companion and get on with his appointed task. The whole affair was very strange. Had she been travelling alone when she was attacked? If so, that was an odd thing. And what was she doing so far from her own home? It seemed to him unlikely that he would ever learn the answers to these questions.

While he was turning over in his mind the implications of making a detour to see this young woman safely home, Sykes saw that there was a party of riders in front of them, coming along the road in their direction. He took out the field glasses and found that there were half a dozen Indian warriors heading straight for them. He supposed that they might be something to do with the woman he had rescued, but it might equally well be the case that they were from another tribe and would turn out to be enemies of them both.

Suddenly the woman riding at his side urged on her pony and went cantering towards the men. Colonel Sykes reined in and waited to see what would chance. It was plain that these were relatives or friends of the girl, because they greeted her with shouts of pleasure. There followed a long conversation, during the course of which the girl gestured in his direction and all the men stared towards him. Well, he thought to himself, I had best see how the land lies. He trotted on towards the group, eyeing them warily. As he drew nigh to them, the men all raised their open palms in a greeting that indicated peaceful intentions.

'Well,' said Sykes, 'I don't know if any of you boys understand me, but your friend here was in difficulties, from which I extracted her. But I am in a powerful hurry now and if you will give me the road, I needs must bid you farewell.'

The woman said, 'Thank you,' and the men inclined their heads slightly in acknowledgement.

He trotted forward and they made way for him. Then the whole strange adventure was over and he was trotting alone down the road towards Cejita de los Comancheros.

CHAPTER 3

Colonel Sykes camped that night a little off the road. Although it was chilly he decided against a fire. He had been able to obtain some meagre rations from the kitchen at Camp Edgewood, but there had been no coffee to spare. He ate sufficient of the bread, cheese and ham, leaving a little for the morning. Then he laid out his blanket and stretched himself out to sleep.

He lay looking up at the stars for quite a time, trying to make some sense of his feelings. The predominant emotion which he had felt since leaving the base was one of sheer exhilaration at being in the saddle once more and setting off to undertake a dangerous mission. This was what he had been made for, the only real life he had known since school. Farming had never had any attraction for him and the last year, since the end of the war, had been slow torture. He saw the years stretching bleakly before him; years, decades even, in which he grubbed out a living from the earth.

He hated everything about farming; from the dirt which found its way under his immaculately kept fingernails to the uncertain ways of growing crops and their tendency to behave in alarming ways, dropping dead a week before being ready to harvest. How any man could devote his life to such an enterprise, the colonel could not conceive. It was soul-destroying and back-breaking and he would be damned if he was going to take it up again after this little jaunt. He would sell up and find another line of work: something more in keeping with his own special talents. Although what the devil that might be was anybody's guess. Having made this decision, Sykes felt a little easier in his mind and gradually drifted off to sleep.

When he awoke the next day the colonel felt a lot more cheerful for having made up his mind about the future course of his life. For now, though, he needed to get a line on this girl whom he was to free from captivity and the only way to do that would be to fall in with some of the comancheros who traded around this part of the territory. If his memory did not play him false, there was a little town some ten or fifteen miles ahead, the name of which he could not call to mind offhand. It was at a crossroads and the cantina there was a clearing house for gossip and information. Unless things had changed greatly over the course of the last three or four years he would be sure to find out something there. Mind, he thought, it is entirely possible that it does not even exist any more. The whole town could have been destroyed in the fighting. We shall see.

Fortunately, the town looked to be more or less intact as Colonel Sykes rode into it. Even the cantina, which he recalled so vividly, seemed just as he remembered it. There was nobody much about, it still being early morning, so Sykes dismounted and led his horse along the main, indeed only, street of the town. It was then that he had one of those rare strokes of good fortune which from time to time strike a man like random lightning. There was a shout from across the street. He ignored it, assuming that nobody in this place would be likely to recognize or remember him. The cry was repeated and this time he heard his own name:

'Sykes, you bastard, won't you say hallo to an old friend?' Looking closely at the man ambling across the road towards him, Colonel Sykes realized with a sudden shock that here was somebody he had once known very well indeed.

When the Confederate forces were advancing along the Rio Grande into New Mexico in February 1862, Sykes had been attached to General Sibley's staff. One of the other officers on the staff was a fellow called Captain Hunter. Although they only fought side by side for a couple of months, the two men had felt a kind of rapport and were both sorry to part when their duties separated them. He had often wondered what had become of Jack Hunter and now here he was, in the very same area where they had campaigned together.

Sykes held out his hand to the approaching man and said in a correct and formal manner, 'Captain

Hunter, I believe?'

'Believe that and you'll believe anything, my boy. Did you not hear that I finished the war a major?'

'I stand corrected. I am delighted to see you again, *Major* Hunter.'

'Likewise, I'm sure. I'm not apt to make the same error about rank as you did just now. The reputation of Colonel Thomas Sykes has even reached us down here in the wilds.'

Behind the banter was the genuine pleasure of the two men in encountering each other again. Sykes said, 'What are you doing here, Hunter? You live here or what?'

'Live here? In San Diablo? No sir, not a bit of it. I am on my way south to make my fortune. What about you? What brings you here?'

'That's by way of being a long story. Is there some place we could talk?'

'Why surely. I have a room over the cantina. It's only small, but I am only here for a day or two before I move on. It's the hell of a chance that you found me here. That's to say, if it *is* chance?' Hunter looked enquiringly at his old comrade.

'For aught I know to the contrary, Hunter, chance is all it is. I am only passing through this way myself.'

The other man looked as though he expected Colonel Sykes to elaborate a little on what he was up to, but when it became clear that he wasn't about to do so, Hunter led him towards the cantina.

There was nobody in the little bar room at such an early hour, so Hunter thought that they might as well

talk there. He ordered a snack and some cold but-
termilk. Neither of them felt like drinking hard
liquor before noon. When they were settled down in
a corner, Colonel Sykes said, 'You say you're heading
south. By which I take it you mean Mexico?'

'You got that right. I won't fox with you, Sykes. I
have been offered a commission in the forces of
Juàrez, who looks to be the next leader of the
country, once they have turfed out the French and
deposed that so-called emperor of theirs. Yes sir,
Juàrez is the man to stick to. He is building up a
proper army, and getting in on the ground floor, as
you might say, means that when he takes power in a
year or so, why then Major Jack Hunter will be ready
to rise quickly.'

'If you live that long. I heard that the fighting is
pretty lively.'

'Yes, but here's the good bit. The Yankees are
supplying Juàrez with arms and everything else he
needs. With Uncle Sam on his side, I can't see how
he can lose. Still, enough about me. What brings you
here?'

'That's no great mystery. I'm trying to make
contact with some of the comancheros up on Cejita
de los Comancheros. Can you set me on the right
path?'

'Well, you know the way there well enough, same
as I do. This talk of setting you on the right path
means that you are looking for an introduction of
some sort, is that the way of it?'

'That's about the strength of it, yes,' said Colonel

Sykes. 'I wish to make contact with the comancheros.'

'Man alive!' said Hunter. 'But what do you want to do a thing like that for? You know what a set of cut-throats those fellows are. I mind that you speak Spanish and all, but even so, they'll be taking you for a spy or some such.'

When Sykes said nothing his friend looked alarmed, saying, 'Hey you're not, are you? Acting the part of a spy or anything of that sort?' The colonel gave him an indignant look and Hunter went on hurriedly, 'Sorry, I didn't really think it for a moment, but won't you tell me what you are really doing out here?'

Colonel Sykes said nothing for a space, then remarked, 'I reckon it's time we both showed our hands. I will lay down first and you can see how the case sits.' He gave a brief account of the events that had led to his fetching up here in San Diablo. Hunter in turn explained how things stood from his standpoint.

'Here's how it is, Sykes. I have been riding with some comancheros myself. We have been running guns to the redskins and very profitable it has been, too. To speak bluntly, I've not been able to settle down since the surrender. Whether I miss the excitement or if it's just that I don't care for the reconstruction, one way and another I couldn't just sit peacefully at home. So I came down here and have been having some rare fun, raiding the Yankees for guns, among other things.'

'Why are you leaving now to go to Mexico?' asked

Sykes curiously, 'Why not carry on as you are?'

'Because the game's played out, is why. The army are ready to come down on us like a duck on a June bug and I wouldn't care to be around when that happens. They're driving the Kiowa and Comanche on to reservations and they aren't none too keen on our interference. The last straw came a week ago.'

'How's that?'

Three men entered the little cantina and nodded amiably to Hunter. He smiled back briefly and then said in a low voice, 'I don't feel much like discussing this here. Not with others present. Let's you and me go for a stroll.'

The two men walked out into the bright spring sunshine. It surely was a beautiful day. A fifteen-minute walk took them to the edge of town and they wandered up towards the hills that ringed the little settlement. When they were completely clear of the place Hunter said, 'We, which is to say me and the comancheros, are in the habit of getting hold of guns and selling them to the Kiowa and Comanche.'

'Which I already knew,' observed Colonel Sykes. 'Profitable and not too strenuous, I should say.'

'Just so. Lately, the army have been 'losing' guns to Juàrez and his men. They take 'em down to the Rio Grande, signal the Mexicans and then withdraw and let them be taken. We've been shadowing them and jumping in first. Snatching the rifles and then trading them to the Comanche. The army have been getting a mite ticked off with us, I don't mind telling you.'

'You surprise me,' said Sykes drily.

'Well, last week things came to a head, only it wasn't none of our doing. Someone in Washington decided to let the rebels in Mexico have something a little bigger. They sent ten brand-new Gatling guns down to the border. Only thing is, they never got that far. Band of Comanches ambushed them and seized the things. Killed all the soldiers in the process, of course. They've no use for Gatlings, so they traded them on to a bunch of comancheros, who are planning to sell them to Juàrez. The army are mightily displeased and are going to be coming down this way any time to recover those guns at any cost. This is not going to be a healthy location when that happens.'

This was the worst possible news for Colonel Sykes. All his plans had been predicated upon the assumption that he would be dealing only with a set of outlaws and that these would be the only force to reckon with. That the regular army was heading here at any moment made his task immeasurably more difficult. If they *were* holding any hostages the comancheros would be sure to dispose of them as quickly as possible and then hide the evidence. The army would have a short way with anything that looked at all like slave-trading. He would have to move very fast and hope to find the girl and remove her before the fighting began. If they were to be caught in a three-way battle between the army, the comancheros and various Indians, the chances of either himself or the girl making it out alive were slender indeed.

'I suppose that this is why a commission in Juàrez's army is suddenly an attractive prospect?' said Sykes.

'Just so. As for your own affair, I have heard nothing about this girl. She could be round here or she might not be. I have an idea of where she might be, though, and that is Fort Bennett.'

'What's that, a town?'

'No, it's an old army fort, on the edge of the plateau. It was abandoned after the war and a bunch of men under the leadership of one who calls himself Don Jose moved in and took it over. I don't know if you'd call them comancheros or just bandits. I hear they have young women there from time to time, who they either ransom back to their families or sell across the border.'

'Can you tell me how I can get to this place?'

'I can do better than that,' said Hunter. 'I can introduce you to some of the men who live there. If we represent the case in the right light they might be induced to take you there.'

By the time they returned to it, San Diablo's cantina was filling up with a variety of rough-looking types. At a guess Sykes would have said that most of them were either outlaws or as close to it as made no odds. All were heavily armed and they had the air of men who did not carry guns just for show. The majority of those in the bar were, by the look of it, of Spanish or Indian ancestry. Colonel Sykes felt that he would fit in easily enough among such fellows, both with his dark complexion and also his ability to speak the language at least as well as a Mexican.

Hunter told the colonel to wait a little while he approached the necessary people and arranged to effect an introduction. After a few minutes he returned and told Sykes to follow him to a corner of the cantina, where three men sat at a table. Colonel Sykes did not much care for the look of them. Still and all, he was hardly in a position to be fussy about the company he kept. He greeted them in Spanish, which caused some consternation. The man who was evidently their spokesman said in the same language, 'We were told that you were a colonel in the Confederate Army. Is it not so?'

'It was so. But I am also Spanish, or at least half Spanish.'

'We hear that you are wanted by the Yankees for the murder of one of their soldiers. Is it so?'

'I killed one of their men, yes.'

'And now you need somewhere to stay before you go to join Juàrez. Is that also true?'

Sykes could not help but admire the skilful way that Hunter had managed to weave together fact and fiction to create the sort of story calculated to arouse sympathy for him in the hearts of a band of unprincipled wretches such as these. He said, 'It is even so.'

The man studied Colonel Sykes's face intently, as though hoping to read there something of his character and essential nature. Then he said, 'You know the old Catalan saying? "One hand washes the other"?'

'I have heard this said,' admitted the colonel cautiously. 'What is this to do with me?'

'We have a little problem. Perhaps if we shelter you from your enemies you will in turn do us some slight service as a return for our hospitality.'

Sykes's heart sank at these words. As if he did not already have enough to demand his attention! And after all this, it might even turn out that the girl he was seeking was not to be found at this Fort Bennett. Still, he did not see that he had another choice, so he inclined his head graciously and murmured, 'Of course. That would be only fair. Might one ask as to the nature of this service?'

'It is a military matter. I cannot say more until we are at our camp and I may present you to Don Jose.'

'When do we leave? If, that is, you consent to my coming with you.'

'In two hours. Meet us here. They call me Carlo.'

Colonel Sykes bowed gracefully and went off with Hunter. Once they had left the cantina he said, 'Any idea what this "service" is that those boys require of me?'

'I didn't understand much of what you were saying; you spoke too fast. I've not the least notion what they want of you. I hope that you know what you're about, Sykes. Those men would cut your throat as soon as look at you.'

'That was how I read it too. Mind, they think that I can help them and that must be worth something.'

'Why don't you drop this business and just come to Mexico with me? It would be like old times, campaigning along the Rio Grande!'

'I can't. I gave my parole that I would undertake this job. I would be a scurvy devil if I just left this girl and didn't try to help her.'

'If you change your mind you can cross over at El Paso. I don't think you'd have much trouble contacting Juàrez's men there. I'm sure there would be a commission waiting for you in his army.'

'I won't deny that it is a tempting prospect. It would be good to be back in the army again.'

'Well, think it over. You want to walk a ways and talk for a bit?'

The two men strolled round, talking of this and that until the time had worn on and Sykes was due to leave with the three comancheros. Hunter showed him where he could buy some provisions, fill his canteens and so on. The horse that he had borrowed from the army did not look any too pleased to have been left standing in the highway for three hours or so, but Sykes hoped to be able to give her a bit of freedom later.

Before he left Hunter gave him a few names to ask for if he found himself able to cross the border at El Paso. As they parted, he said to Colonel Sykes, 'It has been like the old days, meeting you again, Sykes. I truly hope that we might ride together again.'

'It may yet be so, Jack, it may be so.'

The men with whom he was to ride to Fort Bennett

45

were not a talkative bunch. Sykes had taken great and particular care to speak only in very correct Castilian Spanish, which he had learned at his mother's knee. He had given no hint that he was familiar with the strange dialects that were used hereabouts. He did not want anybody to know that he was pretty fluent in the creole that the comancheros spoke among themselves, especially when there were strangers about.

From the late seventeenth century onwards the Hispanic traders of the area that became Texas and New Mexico developed a slang, which was based partly upon low Spanish and partly on the Comanche language. They called this dialect Taibo. It was a way of recognizing a fellow comanchero; two such men could converse pretty freely, even among a group of Spanish speakers, and be pretty sure that nobody would understand what they were talking about.

Now, as they rode along the road, Colonel Sykes could overhear scraps of conversation in Taibo. The gist was that they were pleased to have found a man like him and that, far from doing him a favour by sheltering him, they actually needed his help in some project. What this might be Sykes was unable to hazard even a tentative guess.

The four of them rested for the night in the lee of a little cliff, which rose vertically from the surrounding land. The comancheros lit a fire without any of the hesitation that Sykes had felt about revealing his position the previous night. Perhaps they felt that this was their territory and that any strangers should be more afraid of them than they were of the strangers. They turned in as soon as it was completely dark and the colonel fell asleep almost immediately.

CHAPTER 4

If this Fort Bennett was on the edge of Cejita de los Comancheros they should arrive by late evening. That at least was the calculation that Colonel Sykes made when he woke the next morning. The prospect of spending an entire day in the company of these taciturn men was not an enticing one, but there was little to be done about it.

They rode hard that day, alternating trotting with cantering. There was no more conversation than there had been the previous day. Every so often Carlo would condescend to speak to him in Castilian, but Sykes did not exchange a single word with the other two. They spoke either in Taibo or, at other times, in a debased form of Spanish that might have been spoken in some isolated Mexican village. Sykes could barely understand one word in ten of what they said. All he could pick up was that there was a hurry to reach Fort Bennett and that Don Jose would be pleased with them for bringing the colonel to his stronghold.

The land began to rise, leading up to the plateau for which they were heading. Hardly anybody else seemed to be on the road, which struck Colonel Sykes as a little odd. He knew that many Indians lived in these parts, but there was no sign of them. He wondered if it was because of the efforts being made by the army to herd them into reservations. Maybe it was healthier for them to keep out of sight. At length, just as the sun was dipping below the horizon, they came to the top of a rise of land and the men he was with reined in their horses. Carlo pointed to a huddle of buildings about two miles away and said, 'Fort Bennett.'

It was one of the adobe forts that had been thrown up around here during the war. It was hard to say at this distance, but it looked to be in pretty good shape. Presumably those living there had repaired any damage. That's the beauty of adobe, get any holes or cracks and you just mix up a little mud and slosh it over the imperfections. Huddled around the fort itself was what looked like some kind of shanty town, made up of tents, wickiups and small adobe huts.

'So that's your base, is it?' said Sykes. 'It looks like many such forts that used to be around here.' His companions said nothing and so he continued, 'Before we take a step further, perhaps you men would tell me what this work is that you want me to undertake at yon fort?'

'It is nothing,' said Carlo. 'Some machinery we want to be mended, that is all.'

'I'm no mechanic. I know nothing about machinery. I ask again, what is it about?'

'You have my word that it is nothing that might go against your honour. If you do not choose to help us, then you may walk off and we will say nothing more.'

This did not strike Colonel Sykes as being at all likely. After bringing him to their base, he would be in a very awkward situation were he to decline any request for help and assistance. There it was, though; he had little choice but to go on. Before they continued he said to Carlo, 'I will hold you to your word on this.' It was a meaningless statement, given that he was riding into their very lair, but he wanted the man to know that if there was trouble, then the colonel would be having a personal grudge against him over the business.

They rode on to Fort Bennett. The closer they came, the more the place looked to Sykes's practised eye like an armed camp expecting an attack at any moment. Sentries patrolled the walls of the fort, and everywhere he looked he could see signs of men prepared for battle. What were they worried about, wondered the colonel. An attack from other outlaws? Indians?

The fort itself was a sprawling structure enclosing something like three acres. The adobe walls were stout enough, but only about twelve or fifteen feet high. It was really more like a compound than a fort. From near to the tops of the walls wooden spars projected at intervals of six feet or so. It would be defensible against infantry, but a single field gun would be able to breach the walls in minutes.

There were some proper quarters inside the fort, solid-looking barracks which had been used by the army when they occupied this region, but other than that it was all very makeshift. In the colonel's professional view it would be possible to hold this place against a company or two of infantry, but sappers or artillery would make short work of it.

Nobody took any special notice of Sykes and after they had ridden into the fort Carlo and the other two men went off and left him to his own devices. In addition to the men there were a few women and even one or two children. The women looked to be either Mexican or half-breed Indians. There was certainly nobody around who could pass for the President's niece. Still, that was only to be expected: they would hardly leave their hostages roaming freely round the camp. He would have to investigate a little and see where they might be holding any prisoners.

Colonel Sykes was wandering round in a seemingly casual way, trying to make out the plan of the place, when Carlo came up to him and announced, 'Don Jose will see you at once.'

Sykes was led to what would once have been the base commander's office. Sitting at the desk, probably the very desk left behind by the commander, was a lean and intelligent-looking man dressed all in white. His skin was lighter than Sykes's own and he could have passed for a Northerner without any problem at all. This man rose when Sykes entered the room and held out his hand, saying, 'Colonel Sykes.'

'Don Jose,' Sykes replied. 'It is good to meet you, sir.'

'Sit now and let us talk of how we might help each other. Will you have a glass of whiskey?'

'That would be most welcome. Thank you.'

Carlo left and the two men were alone in the room. In the corner an oil lamp cast its soft yellow light around the room, which was comfortably appointed. There were soft chairs, a cabinet and even a bookshelf full of expensive-looking books standing in one corner. Don Jose saw where the colonel's eyes were resting, and he laughed. 'You are surprised that a comanchero should be reading Cervantes in the evening?'

'Not at all,' said Sykes politely. 'I am fond of Don Quixote myself.'

So far the two of them had spoken English, but now Don Jose said, 'Would you rather we spoke Spanish? I understand that you are proficient in that language.'

'It's one to me,' said Colonel Sykes. 'I speak both well enough.'

'English it shall be, then,' said Don Jose. 'I am always glad of a chance to practise the English tongue. As you might imagine there is little enough opportunity in such a remote location, among my people.'

'Your "people" gave me to understand that you wanted help with some project. They were vague as to the details.'

'Ah yes. That. Come with me, Colonel. Bring your drink by all means.'

There was something a little dreamlike about the scene. The grounds of the fort were illuminated by flaming pine torches and in the dusk it looked to the colonel like a Mexican village. They made their way across the main square, which had once been the parade ground, and arrived at a low building which was guarded by a sentry.

'Our armoury,' said Don Jose, by way of explanation. 'There is a guard for a particular reason, which you shall see.'

Having unlocked the doors to his 'armoury', Don Jose produced a tinderbox and lit a lamp. The room in which Colonel Sykes found himself contained nothing that he could see in the way of guns, swords or other weaponry. There were, simply, large wooden crates stacked against the wall, one of which had been opened and appeared to contain various lengths of metal. He glanced at Don Jose, who said in explanation, 'We have traded and bartered with the Kiowa and Comanche for generations. We swap coffee for ponies, hides for whiskey; I dare say you know about this well enough. Lately, things have been changing. The chief commodity that our Indian friends want is firearms. We provide them with guns and they give us various things in return. Just recently this arrangement was turned on its head, when our friends offered *us* some guns; weapons for which they had no use at all.'

Sykes went over to the crates and looked at the

stencilled markings on them. He turned to Don Jose and said, 'Gatling guns? You must be crazy! The army will quarter this area in search of these. What are you about?'

'It's easy enough to explain, Colonel. We are preparing to leave this fort. The army is making life difficult for us lately and there are perhaps easier pickings to be found now in Mexico itself. But we need a good sum of money first, to establish ourselves elsewhere.'

'You're going to sell the Gatlings? To whom? Juàrez? Why should he buy them from you? The army were giving him these for nothing. What's to stop them getting another dozen and shipping them down to the Rio Grande for the rebels to acquire?'

'I hear that Washington is uneasy about the loss of these guns. The word is out that no more must be hazarded until they can be sure that they are not likely to fall into the wrong hands. That means no more Gatling guns for Juàrez and his army until the Indians are all safely tucked away on reservations. How long do you think that will take? Six months? Nine months? A year? Juàrez needs these now. They could make the difference between victory and defeat for him when he faces Maximilian's troops.'

'You play for high stakes, Don Jose, I will allow. Where do I fit into your little scheme?'

'There are no instructions with these guns which, as you see, are in pieces. We need somebody to show us how to put them together and operate them. Then, if you will, you can come with us to Mexico.'

'I have not exactly made all my plans just yet, but I don't mind helping you with these things.'

'You know about Gatlings?'

'We captured one from the Yankees and took it to pieces. This was a year before the end of the war. There was a plan to start making them in our own factories. Some said that it could have turned the tide of the war, if all our units could have been equipped with such a weapon.'

'What went wrong with the plan?'

'They are too precisely machined. We just didn't have the tools to copy them. Not that it would have made any odds in the long run. Still, that's nothing to the purpose. All you need to know is that I can assemble these and show you how they work.'

'When can you start?'

'If you can rig up some more lamps there's nothing to hinder me from beginning right away.'

'That would be most excellent, Colonel. I shall be sure to have a meal sent to you directly, while you work.'

Sykes was not in the least surprised that Don Jose and his men had been unable to assemble the Gatlings correctly. The construction of the things was not at all like any regular firearm and, unless you were thoroughly familiar with the weapon, it was impossible to guess where each piece fitted. Not least of their peculiarities was that each gun had no fewer than six barrels, each barrel having its own breech and firing mechanism. It was hard enough to work out the action when you had taken one to pieces;

starting from the contents of these crates alone would be like solving some complicated Chinese puzzle.

Whistling tunelessly through his teeth, Colonel Sykes methodically removed the contents of one of the wooden boxes and set out the pieces so that he could remind himself how they fitted together. The gun came with its own spanners and other tools and, once you knew what you were about, the thing was fairly straightforward. Unless you had a mental image or pattern to which you were working, though, the job was fiendishly difficult. For one thing, there were a number of fiddly little springs, which had to be held in place while other parts were inserted. Many a man who had put one of these guns together had been known to remark that a third hand would not have come amiss during some stages of the process.

It was while he was focused fully upon the task in hand and wishing that he had insisted on waiting until the job could be done in broad daylight, that the colonel became aware that he was being watched. He had always had a cat's sense about such things and although he had heard nobody enter the room he knew without the shadow of a doubt that somebody had walked through the door and was now staring at his back. He whirled round and almost dropped the spanner that he had been using to coax a recalcitrant spring into place. A tall, slim white girl was standing casually by the doorway, her eyes taking in the scene with interest. He had not been shown a photograph, but the girl for whom he had come in search had been described to him well enough. Standing only a few feet away was Elizabeth Harper, the President's niece.

Sykes put down the spanner and said, 'Miss Harper, I believe?'

'Say, how do you know my name? Who are you?'

Colonel Sykes lowered his voice, saying, 'Not so loud, Miss Harper. I have come to rescue you.'

'Rescue?' exclaimed the young woman in amazement. 'I don't need rescuing. What are you talking about?'

'Your family have dispatched me here for no other purpose than to bring you safely back to your loved ones,' said Colonel Sykes, a note almost of entreaty entering his voice. 'You need not be afeared.' Already, though, he could pretty much see how things stood. He didn't know the details, of course, but it was tolerably clear to him that this young woman was no sort of prisoner and would not be leaving Fort Bennett until she was good and ready.

'If all this talk of my "loved ones" signifies Uncle Andrew, then you can just dispatch yourself back again and tell him to tend to his own affairs. I'm going nowhere.'

Sykes had no time to say anything further, because at that moment Don Jose walked through the door, bearing a silver tray with half a roast fowl and a bottle of wine. He seemed surprised to see the girl there.

He said chidingly, 'What are you doing here, Elizabeth? Run along now, my guest is too busy to listen to your chattering.' The girl pulled a face, but left at once. 'Enchanting little creature, is she not?' remarked Don Jose.

'Relative of yours, sir?' asked the colonel casually.

'Hardly that. See now, I turn myself into a waiter for you. Here is the meal which I promised.' He set the tray down and then turned his attention to the Gatling gun, which was taking shape under the colonel's capable fingers. 'Ah, you are making good progress. Do you think that you will complete it tonight?'

'I don't see why not. You don't mind if I stop and enjoy that chicken?'

'Why no, that is why I brought it for you. Tell me, how long will it take you to assemble all ten of the guns?'

'Day after tomorrow, perhaps?'

'You cannot work any faster? Matters are reaching a climax and it would be, how shall I say, embarrassing to be caught here if the army arrived unannounced.'

Colonel Sykes rubbed his chin thoughtfully. 'I tell you what. If two of your men were to work alongside me tomorrow and watch what I'm doing, I don't see why we can't set it up like a manufactory, with two or three Gatlings being worked on at once. Would that suit?'

'That would "suit" very well indeed, Colonel.'

'That young lady who was here earlier; she some sort of friend of yours?'

'How delicately you Southern gentlemen speak of

affairs of the heart. "Some sort of friend"! You mean, is she my mistress? I will not weary you with tales of my love life. She is a friend until we leave and then, alas, I must abandon her. I do not think that my wife would take kindly to my arriving home with that young woman in tow.'

'I did not mean to pry.'

'Ah, as to that, do not distress yourself. I must leave you now. There is much to be accomplished before we move from here. We have been here nearly a whole year, you know. Ever since the army deserted this fine building.'

After Don Jose had left Colonel Sykes turned these new developments over in his mind. Two things stood out with unshakable clarity. The first was that that young fool fancied herself in love with the comanchero leader and perhaps was deluded enough to believe that he felt the same way about her. The second point connected with the first: this elegant gentleman was planning to ditch the girl within a day or two.

It was a regular conundrum. How was he, Sykes, to reveal the man's true character to the girl and then persuade her to allow him to rescue her? How had those two met? The more he thought about this, the more convinced did Sykes become that things were not at all as they had been represented to him back in Milledgeville. There was more to this whole business than met the eye.

As he munched on the succulent flesh of the chicken, which had been cooked to perfection, the colonel reflected that nothing involving the fairer sex was ever apt to be straightforward and uncomplicated. With men, you could generally see what their line was and figure out the play. This seldom seemed to be the case with women and despite the fact that it had saved his neck, Sykes felt very much inclined to curse the chance that had caused him to become entangled in this web.

In the meantime the first of the Gatling guns was still not completely assembled and this one would be necessary as a pattern for his assistants to study in the morning. Colonel Sykes was quite confident that if he was given two men of average intelligence, then he would be able to get the other nine guns ready in the course of a single day. Then, he supposed, it would simply be a question of explaining how they were used and perhaps demonstrating one in action.

By eleven that night Sykes had the first gun put together, with the exception of the firing pins. These were nowhere to be found and although he had emptied the crates that contained the other parts, there was no sign of the pins. This was a serious setback, because without the firing pins the weapons were useless. Perhaps they had been carried separately when the guns were being transported. Could those moving them to the border have anticipated some such state of affairs as this and sent the firing pins on a different wagon? He would have to wait until the morning to see. There was little point in peering around in the dim lamplight tonight.

A man put his head around the door and said,

'Don Jose has set a bed for your use. I am to escort you to it.' After he had extinguished the lamps, this fellow locked the door behind them when they left and detailed some poor devil to stand watch at the door for the next three hours.

The bed was comfortable enough and he had a room of his own. All things considered, Colonel Sykes thought that he was probably being treated as an honoured guest. As he lay there, waiting for sleep to overtake him, he wondered once more about Elizabeth Harper. Would she say anything to Don Jose about his mission to rescue her? If so he could perhaps expect to have his throat cut during the night. Sykes had the distinct impression that Don Jose, for all his easy and hospitable ways, would be a very bad man to fall foul of. He would just have to hope that the girl kept her mouth shut until he could find a chance to speak privately to her again.

Just before he fell asleep the colonel decided that there was no percentage in making things too easy for any potential assassin. He climbed out of the bed and dragged it across the room so that it was blocking the doorway, preventing the door from opening. Then he placed his pistol under the pillow and relaxed a little more. There was nothing to stop anybody wishing to kill him from climbing through the window, but he had at least made the task of murdering him just that little bit more difficult.

CHAPTER 5

Colonel Sykes was catapulted from his slumbers by a violent banging and shaking of the bed in which he was sleeping. He grabbed the Colt Army from beneath his pillow and had already cocked the piece with his thumb, before realizing that it was morning and the banging was nothing more sinister than somebody trying to open the door, which he had blockaded with the bed.

'Don Jose sent you this coffee,' said a timid-looking young woman, who had been rattling the door back and forth in an attempt to gain admittance to the room. 'He hopes that you will be up soon.'

'Just a moment,' said Sykes in Spanish. 'I will admit you to my chamber.'

The girl giggled at the colonel's flowery and formal language. The Spanish that most of the people here spoke was a much coarser and earthier form of the language. When once he had pulled the bed away from the door and had made himself look

62

more decent, Sykes invited the young woman into the room. She was only young; a slender, dark-skinned little thing, with a scared look about her.

'Come in, child, and let me speak with you,' said the colonel. 'I would ask you one or two questions.'

'I have a lot to do . . .' said the girl doubtfully.

'Tell people that I delayed you, then.'

Once the girl had brought the jug of coffee and the cup into the room, Sykes closed the door behind her. She gave him a saucy look, as though she understood this to be the prelude to seduction. The colonel was horrified at the idea that she might have placed such a construction upon his actions.

He said hastily, 'You need not fear me. I want only to ask you one or two questions.'

'I do not know anything. Nobody tells me about things.'

'The American girl, Elizabeth Harper. You know something of her?'

'Oh, her!' said the girl contemptuously. 'Everybody knows about her.'

'Well, I don't. What is it that everybody knows?'

'That she is Don Jose's favourite, his pet. She preens herself and puts on airs, as though she were the mistress and not the maid. She treats the rest of us like peons.'

'Does she indeed? How came she here?'

The girl shrugged. 'I heard that they were old friends from when she was a child. They say that she is a high-born one. Is it true?'

'I could not say.'

'If she only knew how many of us have likewise shared Don Jose's bed and then been discarded in turn, I am sure she would be humbled. But it will come to her.'

Colonel Sykes stood and said, 'Thank you, you have been very helpful. There is perhaps no need to repeat what was said here.'

'What, and earn myself a whipping for speaking out of turn? If you need help, I will give it willingly.'

'I am greatly obliged to you. Thank you.'

This was all most perplexing, although some things were becoming plain. For instance, it was certain that Don Jose had known Elizabeth Harper before she had been seized by the Indians. It was equally sure that she did not know of his reputation as a womanizer and that she fancied herself his fiancée or some such nonsense. If he was to persuade her to leave with him it would be necessary for the colonel to have a good long chat and show her how things stood.

His heart sank at the prospect. In his experience, women were remarkably foolish about even the most worthless and vicious of men, if once they felt that they were in love. Like as not, if he spoke bluntly to this girl she would go trotting off to Don Jose and tell him all that had been said. It was a damned nuisance.

Colonel Sykes turned his mind to something a little easier to solve: the matter of the Gatling guns. He would have a last search for the firing pins and then tell Don Jose about this problem. In the meantime, if he really was to be given helpers he could set them to assembling the other weapons while he fiddled around with the fine adjustments.

Idling around outside the building containing the Gatlings were two ill-favoured young men who Sykes knew at once were going to be trouble. He had had to deal in his time in the army with many such men; arrogant young fellows who regarded the simplest instruction as a challenge to their manhood. Let somebody issue an order and men of this type will be sure to either disobey or wilfully misinterpret what has been said, so that they are unable to do as they have been told.

'Good day to you,' said the colonel. 'I hope you are ready to help me to the best of your ability?'

Neither man replied. They just stood there, louring at him, as though awaiting the opportunity to frustrate his orders. *Lord,* thought Sykes to himself, *this is going to be a hard row to hoe and no mistake.*

'Well,' he said, 'If you would give me a hand getting the crates out into the daylight, then we can set to work.' The men did not move. 'You are the men that Don Jose sent to help me, are you not?'

'We are,' said one of the young men. The other just stared at the colonel. Sykes supposed that they were irritated at being told to take orders from a gringo, but he couldn't help that. The three of them hauled the wooden boxes out into the sunshine and Colonel Sykes then endeavoured to explain to the boys the construction of the Gatling gun, by showing them the one that he had almost finished putting together.

'See now,' he said in a chatty and friendly fashion, 'There are six barrels which turn around this central shaft. You turn this crank handle and this brings each barrel round, then opens the breech and closes it when a cartridge is in. Then it fires and as the barrel turns, the empty shell is ejected. Is this all clear?'

One of the men shrugged and the other yawned.

Sykes persisted. 'Not many people know that this gun was invented by a lover of peace. There's a thought! Dr Richard Gatling of Ohio thought that weapons like this would do away with the need for large armies and would eventually make warfare impossible. Can you imagine?'

One of the men hawked and spat, the thick phlegm landing near to Colonel Sykes's foot, a proceeding that roused him to anger.

'Mother of God!' he exclaimed. 'Were you born in a pig pen? What ails the pair of you?' It was looking to the colonel as though he would be called upon to be a little firmer with these lazy young devils. Just as he was about to launch into a fierce, parade-ground dressing-down, the one who had spat muttered in a low but all-too-distinct voice, 'Ah, screw your mother!'

Perhaps he did not think that the colonel, with his very correct and formal Spanish, would even recognize such a vulgar expression; if so, he was greatly mistaken.

'What was that?' said Sykes quietly. 'Did you have something to say touching upon my mother? Say it again.'

Perhaps the boy knew that he had gone too far, because he declined to repeat himself. It was no good, though, because the colonel had been effectually roused. He hauled the young man to his feet, and without further ado slapped him twice across the face, once with his open palm and then with the back of his hand.

He was a game one, that boy, and his response was all but instantaneous. He swung his fist at Colonel Sykes's face as his friend also leaped to his feet to join the fray.

Sykes ducked the blow to his head and caught the boy's arm, twisting him off balance and sending him sprawling to the dirt. As he did so the other young man kicked at his groin. Sykes deflected the foot, but the man's boot still made painful contact with his shin. Meanwhile, the first one was on his feet again and had snatched up a length of metal from one of the dismantled Gatling guns. He advanced towards the colonel, swinging this from side to side as though it were a sword. The second young man also picked for himself a gun barrel from one of the other boxes, then he too began advancing upon Colonel Sykes.

There looked to be a chance of his being seriously injured by these two young fools, and Sykes thought that a little subterfuge was justified. He had a greater end in mind and so must finish this idiotic fight in the quickest way possible. He bolted into the dark interior of Don Jose's 'armoury'. The men gave yells of triumph, obviously thinking that the older man was fleeing from them in terror.

Once he was in the darkened room Sykes turned quickly so that he was standing by the wall and out of sight of the young men when they entered. It was an old, old trick, but then he probably had twenty years' advantage over the two of them.

As the first man entered the building, his metal rod stretched out before him, Colonel Sykes simply grabbed it from his grasp. The young man was standing in the bright sun and entering a dark place. Sykes, on the other hand, was in the dark and looking at targets in full sunlight.

Having taken the rod, he whacked the fellow round the side of the head with it, following up with a hard shove, which sent him stumbling into his companion. Then the colonel burst from the darkness and rushed the other man, knocking him to the ground and cracking him too around the side of the head with the piece of metal. Both of the younger men lay there, dazed and either unable or unwilling to rise and face him further.

'My dear Colonel, what are you doing to my sons? I hope you have not damaged them permanently.' Don Jose was standing there in his immaculate white suit, surveying the scene with a puzzled and quizzical look upon his handsome face. He had spoken the question in a sardonic and good-humoured way, but the colonel hoped that he had not injured the boys too badly. He said, 'You will forgive me for observing, Don Jose, that your boys do not take after you in gentility.'

'Ah,' said Don Jose, his teeth flashing in amusement,

'They are not "chips off the old block"?'

'I would not have said so, no.' Briefly, Sykes outlined the events leading up to the little fracas. After listening gravely, Don Jose spoke a few sharp words to the two young men, who slunk off, giving Colonel Sykes venomous glances that foretold a grudge to be settled at some future and more convenient time.

'A fine pair of ruffians, are they not?' said Don Jose. 'They are the product of one dalliance of mine with a very backward village girl. They are good fighters, but not perhaps overburdened with intellect.'

'I wonder you thought them suitable for helping in this matter.'

'I try to give them greater responsibility. Sometimes it works.'

'Not this time, though.'

'No, not this time. I shall send you a couple of older and more steady men.'

This seemed as good an opportunity as any to apprise Don Jose of the missing firing pins. Sykes said, 'We have a little problem. All the pieces for these guns are here except for the firing pins. I can certainly put the Gatlings together, but without the pins they will be useless.'

A look of consternation crossed Don Jose's face. 'How so? Can you not take pieces from other weapons?'

'Impossible. Look, I'll show you.' Colonel Sykes demonstrated the firing mechanism of the guns, saying, 'Each barrel has its own firing pin. There are ten guns, each with six barrels. We need sixty firing pins to get them all into working order.'

'Have you checked rigorously every crate?'

'No. I was about to do so when your sons and I had that little contretemps.'

'Let us do so now, together. You are quite sure that nothing can be done without them?'

'As I say, we can put the things together, but they won't fire without those pins. Don't think that you can improvise; that won't answer. We tried that during the war, when we were hoping to make our own version of the Gatling.'

The two of them opened every crate and examined every piece of metal contained within them. At the end of their search there was not the least doubt that the firing pins were nowhere to be found.

'This is a confounded nuisance,' said Don Jose. 'There is one chance, and that is that those who took these guns from the cavalry unit also took the firing pins, not recognizing them for what they were. Tell me, would you have expected to find the firing pins just thrown in the boxes along with the other pieces?'

'No, I wouldn't. What's more, they're not listed here on the inventories. Look!' Colonel Sykes handed Don Jose a flimsy sheet of paper which he had uncovered in the bottom of one of the boxes. It read:

THIS BOX CONTAINS
ONE GATLING GUN
Calibre .30

1 Crank Handle and Pin	1 Lock Screw Driver
1 Pointing Lever	1 T Screw Driver
1 Axis Pin, Washer and Nut	1 Small Screw Driver
1 Binder Box, Plate, Screw, Pin, Washer and Key	1 Rear Guide Nut Wrench
2 Guide Ways	1 Cascable Wrench
1 Shell Driver	1 Lever Axis Pin Nut Wrench
1 Wiping Rod (Brass)	

MANUFACTURED BY
Colt's Patent Fire Arms Mfg. Co. Hartford
Connecticut

'Ah, I see. No mention of any firing pins. That suggests to you, my friend, that they were being carried separately?'

'That's about the strength of it,' said Sykes. 'With luck, your Indian friends will have them, but they could have been sent by another consignment entirely.'

'Ach, this is not good. Not good at all. If you will engage to assemble the other weapons, I will send to our allies and see if they have these things. If not, I do not mind confessing to you, I am not sure what we will do.'

'You will let me have a couple of likely fellows, as will not curse and fight with me?'

'Yes, yes, make yourself easy about that. They will be here directly.'

Don Jose was as good as his word. Two older men appeared; they were apt pupils, listening carefully as the colonel explained the construction of the Gatling guns and soon picking up what was required. Together, the three of them laboured in the morning sun until by midday they had put together four of the guns. A crowd gathered to watch them at work, and when the guns were completed Colonel Sykes sent one of the men into the building to fetch out the wheels, which had been stacked separately against the wall. These they fitted to the axle.

When they had finished there were four brand-new Gatling guns such as few armies in the world could have boasted of. One man with a Gatling could, with luck, hold off a troop of cavalry. Sykes very much feared that these monsters would change the face of warfare for all time when once they became common on the battlefield.

They had left the ammunition boxes inside, because Colonel Sykes was a stickler for safety and did not belive in bringing together guns and ammunition unless you were proposing to start shooting. Nevertheless, he wanted to be sure that the shells fitted into the chambers without any difficulty, so he sent one of the men to bring him a handful of the ammunition.

He needn't have worried. Everything worked perfectly; he even ventured to test the extractor by turning the crank handle a couple of times. If and when the firing pins could be located Don Jose would be able to command his own price for these guns from Juàrez and his rebels.

After a light lunch the three of them carried on with their work. Sykes went to relieve himself in one of the old army latrines; when he came out it was to find Elizabeth Harper standing there, apparently waiting to speak to him.

'May I help you, Miss Harper?' he said politely.

'I reckon you don't think that Don Jose is serious about me. Is that it?'

'I know damned well he isn't. For one thing he's married, and for another he has made whores of half the women in this place.' The girl flushed crimson at such plain language, but Colonel Sykes did not feel that it was time to mince his words. 'When they pull out of this place he will discard you like a . . . well, like something for which he has no further use.'

'Some of them girls look at me like I'm nothing special. I wondered about it. When I first met Jose it was different. I was at school, you know, and he seemed so romantic. Like a bandit leader.'

'He's that all right,' said Sykes grimly. 'Tell me now, will you let me help you escape from this place? You had best make up your mind.'

'I can't say now. I will tell you later. It's a big step.'

'Big step? Why, you young fool, it's the chance of saving yourself. I tell you now, there is going to be some pretty hot fighting round here soon, if Colonel Thomas Sykes is any judge of such matters.'

'Say, are you a colonel? You look too young. I

always think of colonels as being crusty old things.'

Colonel Sykes saw that his two assistants were watching him. He said, 'It's not safe to draw attention to ourselves in this way. I am like to be here until these men break camp. If you have the sense God gave a goat, then you will throw in with me and I will engage to get you clear of here and back home. I can't force you, though.'

Sykes rejoined the two men and started work again. They kept at it throughout the afternoon, and at about five Don Jose came striding across the parade ground with an army satchel in his hands. When he reached Sykes he handed this to him, saying, 'I think these are what you need?'

The colonel unbuckled the leather bag and drew out two or three small objects, each neatly wrapped in greased paper.

'These are the boys, all right,' he said, turning to open the breechblock of one of the Gatlings. The firing pin fitted a treat. 'So they had them all along. Did they know their value?'

The other man pulled a sour face. 'I should say so, yes. They struck a hard bargain for them, so I suppose that they knew we needed them.'

'What sort of bargain?' asked Sykes curiously.

'Ach, that does not signify. It is enough that we have them now. Will you be able to lay on a demonstration of the gun, say this evening?'

'I don't see why not, you know. Give me an hour to make sure that everything is in order. I've only pressed the firing pin into position, but they must all be properly secured. Fire this now and you'll break the mechanism. These are delicate and temperamental beasts. Not like some old musket.'

Colonel Sykes and the two comancheros worked on steadily. From time to time Don Jose came and watched them at work, talking in a relaxed and friendly way with the colonel.

'I think,' he said on one of these occasions, 'I think that with these at his disposal, Juàrez will sweep through the French forces. If, that is, they have not been withdrawn from the country before then, which looks likely.'

'Strikes me that you know a good deal about what is taking place in Mexico,' remarked Sykes. 'You must keep in close contact.'

'My wife and children are there,' said Don Jose. 'At least, my legitimate children, that is to say. I have a mind to retire to an estate there. I am growing too old for this way of life. But first I must ingratiate myself with the new leaders.'

'You seem pretty sure that Juàrez will come out on top,' said Colonel Sykes.

'Juàrez? Yes, he will be the winner, of that I have no doubt at all. You should have volunteered for his forces. He wanted men like you.'

'Should have? Have you forgotten that I am going south with you when you leave here?'

For a moment Don Jose looked discomfited, as though he had been caught out in a lie. Then he recovered himself and said, 'Of course. It slipped my mind.'

Colonel Sykes continued to fix in the firing pins and made sure that his face betrayed nothing, but he was disturbed. Unless he was greatly mistaken Don Jose was not expecting him to go south to Mexico after leaving Fort Bennett. And why that should be, Sykes had not the faintest notion.

CHAPTER 6

It was gone six before the last of the Gatling guns was completely ready for action. Colonel Sykes dry-fired all ten of them a few times, cranking the handles and watching the breeches of the multiple barrels opening and closing. They all appeared to be in perfect condition. With the amount of ammunition which was stacked up in the nearby building, Juàrez's army would be an unstoppable force in Mexico. Don Jose came up just as Sykes had finished testing the last of the weapons.

He said, 'Are you ready to show us how effective these are?'

'That I am, sir. We can't test them in this compound, though. What about wheeling one outside and finding a mark to fire against?'

'A splendid idea, Colonel.' Don Jose gave a word of command and three men began hauling a Gatling across the parade ground and towards the front gate of the fort. It was as awkward and unwieldy to manoeuvre as an artillery piece, with its high, spoked wheels and levers sticking out at unexpected angles.

'There is an old, lightning-blasted tree not far from here,' said Don Jose. 'That might make a good target. You have ammunition?'

'I have enough for a first test-firing, yes,' said the colonel, whose pockets were bulging with .30 shells. 'Mind, at two hundred rounds a minute, I only have enough for a few seconds.'

'It can fire two hundred rounds each minute?' said Don Jose in amazement. 'I never heard the like.'

'The beauty of it is the gravity-fed magazine,' explained Colonel Sykes. 'As fast as you can feed in the cartridges, that's nigh on as fast as you can fire. In the field you would have a team of two, with one man just loading it as you go.'

'Is there no danger of its overheating?'

'No, that's the advantage of having those six barrels. They fire in turn, so each barrel gets a good rest between shots. It can't overheat, no matter how fast you turn the crank.'

Nearly everybody in the fort and the surrounding buildings turned out to follow the Gatling. There was indeed a bare tree about a quarter-mile from the fort. Colonel Sykes directed the Gatling gun to be set up fifty yards from this. Then he made sure that everything was in order. The mechanism had been greased on leaving the factory and so was in wonderful condition. He placed the shells carefully into the hopper at the top of the barrels, checking that they were all lying side by side and ready to slip down into the breeches as the crank was turned.

Then he turned to Don Jose and said, 'This boy makes a fair racket; maybe some would wish to cover their ears.'

This amused Don Jose, who said, 'My people have heard enough gunfire in their time. Come, show us what this marvel can achieve.'

Sykes took a hold of the aiming lever and lined up the sight with the dead tree. Then, without more ado, he began cranking the handle. The noise was unbelievable, like a platoon of infantry all firing at once. He maintained a steady rate of fire, with the result that each successive shot blended into the one before, producing a sound like rolling thunder. The effect on the tree was every bit as impressive as he had hoped.

The first bullets slammed into the old tree, sending splinters of dry wood flying off in all directions. Colonel Sykes tried to keep the fire concentrated in the same part of the trunk and then let it sweep back and forth a few times. The trunk was severed six feet from the ground and, after a few more shots, it toppled sideways, as neatly as though it had been subjected to the attentions of a skilled lumberjack.

'Bravo!' cried Don Jose. 'You will put the men with axes out of business, Colonel. It is the neatest thing I ever saw in my life.'

Just at that moment the Gatling gun ran out of cartridges and Sykes stopped turning the handle. Then he turned in great good humour, like a showman who has undertaken a spectacular feat and is now ready to receive the crowd's applause. Instead, he found that three of the men nearest to him had rifles to their shoulders, which were pointing straight at him.

Don Jose said in Spanish, 'One of you good people be so kind as to remove his gun.' Somebody came up and took the Colt from Sykes's belt.

'What is the meaning of this, you treacherous hound?' said the colonel angrily. 'I thought that we were working to the same end.'

Don Jose said admiringly, 'Even now, when your hand is laid down and found to contain nothing worth noting, you do not give up. You are a remarkable man, Colonel, and I wish that matters had not ended so.'

Five minutes later, Colonel Sykes was sitting in Don Jose's office. He was covered by a tough-looking man who kept his pistol in his hand and didn't take his eyes off the colonel for a second.

'Will you have a last glass of wine with me, before you leave?' asked Don Jose.

'Leave? Where am I going?'

'Alas, you are going to your death, Colonel Sykes, and a most unpleasant death it will be, too. I am sorry; I liked you.'

'Would you care to tell me why you are betraying the custom of hospitality in this way?' asked Sykes coldly. 'Not that I should have expected any more from a brigand, and one who is a libertine into the bargain.'

'You talk to me of betraying hospitality? Curious.

Shall I tell you what first set my suspicions running?'

'If you will.'

Don Jose lifted up from the floor, where it had lain hidden, the small keg of powder which he had brought from Camp Edgewood.

'Do you see the markings on this small barrel?' asked Don Jose. 'You are a professional soldier, you must have noticed before that the army has a positive mania for marking everything it owns? Look here, at the numbers written here. This powder only arrived at Albuquerque two weeks ago. How did you acquire it?'

'I don't ask how you acquire such things as Gatling guns and yet you are now cross-questioning me about five pounds of black powder. I call that rich!'

'Yet you will not or cannot answer my question.'

'This is a heap of foolishness,' said Sykes. 'You are not the only thief in New Mexico, Don Jose.'

'You did not steal this. None of this batch has yet left any of the camps. I know; it is my business to know about such things. This came straight from the stores of, where, Camp Edgewood? You were given it, Colonel. Why?'

'Well,' said Colonel Sykes, 'you have me over a barrel, as they say. However, it looks to me as though our plans damned near coincide and I don't think that we need to fall out. I have done you one favour and now I can do you another.'

'Go on; I am interested.'

'The family of that girl you are fooling around with has hired me to bring her safely home. You said that you were planning to abandon her when you left this fort. Well, let me just take her home. We will be quits.'

Don Jose poured two more glasses of wine from a carafe and handed one to the colonel. He sat for a minute or so, with a sad look upon his face. At last he said, 'I'm afraid it won't work, Colonel. You see, as a comanchero, I make my living from buying and selling. Today, I sold you.'

'Sold me?' asked Colonel Sykes in surprise. 'Who would wish to buy me?'

'It is a long story, but I feel that I owe it to you to explain. Before I do so, I may as well tell you that I have decided against abandoning young Elizabeth after all. She shall go across the border with us, and once there, I shall ransom her to her family. I think that that old fool Johnson will pay handsomely for his relative.'

'You know who she is?'

'Of course I know,' said Don Jose. 'I was acquainted with the young lady two years ago, when she was at school in Houston. She had a passion for me, which I, being so much older, did not encourage. I don't know which of us was more surprised when the Comanche traded her on to us. We knew each other at once.'

Colonel Sykes listened courteously to this, then said, 'None of which explains why I have to die. Could you not just turn me loose?'

'Well, now we come to it. The Comanche have a festival at this time of year, a celebration at which they traditionally sacrifice somebody to ensure that the hunting will be good and similar nonsense. It falls roughly at the same time as our Easter. Really, they are more superstitious than my Catholic family! The death of this sacrificial victim is an agonizing one. The victims arms are bound to his or her side and a long vine is tied round the person's neck. The other end of the vine is secured to a post driven deep into the ground.'

'I had no idea that your interests extended to anthropology, my dear sir. Really, you are more cultured than I could have guessed.'

'I'm glad that you are taking it with such stoicism, Colonel. Anyway, this sacrifice is then tormented. All the tribe jab at him with sharp objects and use torches to burn him. He runs furiously from them, like a bear being baited. Death can take up to four hours to arrive.'

'I take it that I am to be the star performer at such an entertainment?'

'Indeed, yes,' said Don Jose. 'The Comanche had those firing pins and would not part with them until I promised to send them somebody for their vine dance. I knew this morning that you were not precisely as advertised and so the easiest solution was to sacrifice you. I'm sorry, but there it is.'

Colonel Sykes gave no indication at all of his intentions, merely uttering a short, wry laugh. Then he jumped to his feet and dived across the desk, hoping to pluck Don Jose's pistol from where it nestled in the holster at his side. He didn't make it across the desk, though, because the man watching him was prepared for this very move. He was upon Sykes in an instant and swiftly clubbed him into oblivion.

When the colonel came to he was seated on his horse, with his wrists bound together. His head felt vile, as though he had the worst hangover of his whole, entire life, combined with a bout of heat-stroke and the ague. He had no recollection of being mounted upon the horse. As he recovered his senses a little he became aware that he was at the centre of a small cluster of men near to the fort's entrance.

Don Jose was overcoming some remonstrance from a man to his left. Sykes saw to his horror that it was one of the Spaniard's sons: the one he had cracked round the head with the metal rod. This man too was mounted on horseback and Sykes realized that he was to be escorted by this fellow to wherever it was that he was going. This boded ill for his future welfare. He glanced to the right and saw the other son sitting on a horse. When this man saw that Colonel Sykes was awake he gave him an evil leer that suggested that there was to be some sort of reckoning for the bruises which he had given the two youngsters.

The argument seemed to be about his belongings: the Springfield rifle, black powder, pistol and so on. The two boys wanted to keep these things for them-selves, but Don Jose insisted that all should be handed over to the Comanche with the prisoner as a goodwill gesture. It seemed to Sykes that he and all his possessions were being given in payment for the firing pins.

Don Jose was not a man used to being crossed and the boys sullenly agreed that they would hand over all the weaponry, along with the colonel. Don Jose came round to bid him farewell.

He said, 'I truly wish that matters might have taken another course, my dear Colonel. But there it is; we shall not meet again. I only hope that your death is not as prolonged as some of which I have heard.'

Sykes stared at the comanchero leader and said softly, 'I will be back, Don Jose. I will be back, and when I return I will kill you. Don't doubt it.'

'Perhaps. What will be, will be. For now, farewell.'

The party left Fort Bennett at a walk, Don Jose's sons riding on either side of Colonel Sykes. None of the three men spoke a word: for twenty minutes they just walked on in this fashion. When they were completely out of view of the fort the two young men halted their horses and turned to Sykes. Their Spanish was fairly literate, not at all like the weird dialect spoken by the Mexicans and half-breeds.

'We far enough from the fort now?' one said to his brother.

'Surely,' replied the other. 'Nobody can see us from here.'

'We must not damage his legs. If he does not give good sport the Indians will complain to Pa and we'll catch it hot.'

'There's much we can do, without touching his legs.'

None of this made very pleasant listening for a

man whose wrists were lashed together with leather
thongs. Colonel Sykes was weighing up the merits of
spurring his horse into a sudden and unexpected
gallop, when he was overtaken by events. One of the
boys jumped down from his horse and grabbed at
Sykes, pulling him down, to land hard on the rocks.
A curse word escaped Sykes's lips involuntarily, then
the two of them were upon him.

At first the colonel tried to defend himself with his
feet, lashing out hard at any part of the boys' bodies
that came into range. Then one of them drew his
gun and began pistol-whipping the colonel around
the head. Coming on top of the beating he had
already received earlier, this had the effect of making
him giddy and sick. Once they were sure that his
resistance was ended, the two of them beat him
methodically, being careful to avoid harming his
arms and legs. There was a snapping in his mouth
and Sykes realized that they had knocked out at least
two of his teeth.

Eventually the two of them ceased beating him,
possibly because they were out of breath, rather than
for reasons relating to mercy or compassion. As he
lay there, he heard one of them say, 'Mother of God,
look at the state of him. I hope the Comanches won't
tell tales to Pa. He'll kill us.'

'It'll be fine. I dare say he can run well enough.
Let's get him back on the horse.'

'You want that we should take his gun after all?
Maybe Pa won't find out.'

'No, we hand everything over to them. It's a

special gift from Pa. It's a question of face.'

Following this exchange one of the young men booted the colonel in the ribs. The kick struck him where one of his ribs had already been cracked during their attack and the pain was so sickening that he thought he might faint. The boy who had delivered this final assualt leaned over him and said, 'Next time you meet us, you be sure not to hit us, you hear me?' He laughed and continued, 'Oh, wait, I forgot. You won't be meeting us again. Because you will soon be dead. Well, it is something to remember, in any case.'

They had mauled Colonel Sykes so badly that he was quite unable to mount his horse. The boys cursed him, slapped him around and issued the direst threats, but it was all to no avail. In the end, they simply trussed him up like a hog and laid him over the saddle, passing a rope from his wrists and under the belly of the horse to his ankles, so that he would not fall off. As they set out again, Sykes began to pass in and out of consciousness, much to the consternation of the two boys. He gathered from their conversation that there would be hell to pay if he was not fit enough to run and jump vigorously when the Indians were torturing him to death the next day.

The journey to the Comanche village was a nightmare, with Sykes becoming almost delirious with pain. He had no idea how long they continued riding after he was attacked. It was impossible to judge because he kept fainting and then coming to again. The moon was high in the night sky when he saw some twinkling lights ahead of them. He closed his eyes again and when next he opened them, they were entering the village, which consisted of dozens of tepees. It looked like a fair-sized settlement by Indian standards.

The three riders were the object of some little interest, with everybody crowding round and staring curiously at the sight of the half-dead man slung over a saddle like a deer that has been brought home from a hunt. The men who had brought him there seemed to Sykes to be demanding that he be handed over to some particular person and there was some ill-tempered debate when this individual could not at once be located.

After a space, the crowds parted to reveal a chief making his stately way towards the three riders. He came up to Colonel Sykes and looked at him closely. What he saw evidently did not meet with his approval, because he had some sharp words for Don Jose's sons. The young men just shrugged and brushed aside whatever questions were asked of them. Sykes figured that the Comanche chief was probably saying something along the lines of, 'What the hell do you mean by bringing me something in this condition? Fat lot of use this will be for our festival!'

The ropes linking his wrists to his ankles were cut and the colonel was dumped unceremoniously on the ground. If this had been a dime novel, thought the colonel, now would be the time for him to seize a rifle from some nearby warrior, leap on a pony and hightail it out of the village with a posse of redskins in hot pursuit. Then he would jump some wide chasm to safety. In reality, he knew that he could not even get to his feet unaided, never mind about escaping.

Sykes felt, rather than heard, the vibration of the horses' hoofs as the two men left the Indian village. He lay at the centre of a ring of curious faces, wondering when the torment would begin. He had an idea that it would not be until the following day, but there was nothing to stop the Indians from having a bit of fun with him now. Whether or no, he could not move to save his life, so he simply continued to lie there, letting events take their course.

Even in his agony and despair he managed to smile at the thought of what poor sport the Comanches would have with him if they started their infernal vine dance right this minute. He would surely not be doing any jumping and running for their amusement.

Strong arms lifted him to his feet and he was vaguely aware of being carried to a tepee and laid on the floor. Then he knew no more and passed into a state which was to begin with delirium, changing after a while into natural and welcome sleep.

CHAPTER 7

Sykes felt as though he had been kicked all over when he woke the next day. Mind, he thought ruefully, since that was pretty much what *had* happened, it should come as no surprise that he felt that way. The inside of the tepee was cool and dark and he felt no inclination to move for a while. He was very thirsty and not a little hungry, but had no idea whether or not the Indians would think it worth giving him anything to eat and drink if they were planning to kill him that day. He sat up gingerly and figured that apart from a couple of cracked ribs, he was more or less intact. His mouth was swollen and he had a gap where a couple of teeth had been knocked out but, all things considered, he could have been in much worse shape.

From the light filtering through the flap of the tent Colonel Sykes calculated that the sun had risen an hour or so earlier. That meant that he probably had at least another four hours to live. From what he apprehended, the Indians in these parts carried out their most important ceremonies at dawn, midday and dusk. He recalled Don Jose saying something about a victim lasting four hours at the vine dance and that suggested that it began when the sun was at its highest in the sky.

It cannot fall to many men to find themselves, in effect, in two different condemned cells in the space of a week. That, however, was effectively how the case stood. Having already steeled himself to die on the gallows at Milledgeville, Colonel Sykes did not perhaps view the present unhappy set-up from quite the same perspective as the average citizen. He had resigned himself to death a few weeks ago and so he did not feel quite the bitterness about the affair that many a man might have done in his situation.

Try as he might, the colonel could not see any way out of this present bind. Nobody other than the comancheros knew that he was here, the Indians had no reason to spare him, and they seemingly needed a sacrifice this day. From all points of view this was likely to be the final day of his life, which was a melancholy reflection.

The entrance to the tepee was pulled aside and two young men stooped down and entered. They were carrying a birch-bark pail of water and a wooden bowl of some mess of vegetables and beans. They handed this to the colonel and watched impassively as he ate the food ravenously, scooping it up with his hands, which were still tied together. When he had eaten his fill and drunk plenty of water to wash it down with, the braves washed him, wiping away the dried blood from his face. They did this impersonally, as one would tend to an animal. When they had finished, they left the tepee, still without a word, and Sykes was abandoned once more to his own thoughts.

Surpringly, in view of the desperate situation in which he found himself, he dozed off to sleep again. He was woken an hour or more later, by two more braves coming into the tepee. Their job was, as far as the colonel could make out, to prepare him for his ordeal and make him look presentable to the onlookers. They shaved him with an iron blade and dressed his hair with some foul-smelling pomade. After this was done they tended to his fingernails, filing them neatly with a chunk of sandstone.

The final stages of the preparation entailed Sykes's face being painted with some sort of coloured gum. They undertook this task with tremendous dedication, working carefully at their designs with little brushes made of frayed twigs. Colonel Sykes had the grotesque feeling of being an honoured client in some establishment dedicated to the grooming of gentlemen.

The food and water had had the effect of perking up Colonel Sykes and making him feel that some opportunity might yet present itself for him to escape the gruesome fate that lay before him. Perhaps the young men who had been detailed to attend to his needs and beautify him sensed this, because there was no question now of leaving him alone in the tepee. One of them drew a knife and cut his bonds, but the other held him by the arm while this was being done and both watched him like hawks. They were half his age and in superb condition; there was no chance that he would be able to defeat either of them in a fight, considering the state he was in. Tackling both at once was an absurd idea.

Outside the tepee somebody had begun a loud chant. Others took up the refrain, until it put the colonel in mind of the monks he had once heard at a monastery, singing psalms in Latin. He guessed that religious ceremonies like this have a similar sound in many different cultures. The two men, whose job it semed to be to accompany him, urged Sykes to his feet and then opened the flap of the tepee. They stepped out into brilliant sunshine; the sun being, as far as the colonel was able to gauge, at its highest point in the sky.

The bright sunshine dazzled him at first, after the gloomy interior of the tent, and it took a little while for Sykes to get his bearings. The village itself looked to be deserted; there was literally not a soul to be seen. The two men gripping his arms urged him to walk between the tepees and so they traversed the whole settlement, still without setting eyes upon a single person. The explanation for this became apparent when they had reached the edge of the Comanche village.

A vast, saucer-shaped depression in the rocky plain lay some hundred yards from the village. This natural, geological feature was perhaps 300 or 400 hundred feet across and it looked to Sykes like an old-time Roman amphitheatre.In the precise centre of this depression was a post, driven into the ground. Around this, every single inhabitant of the Indian village squatted or sat. The colonel noticed with a thrill of horror that every person held in their hands an implement of some sort. These ranged from lances and spears to sharpened sticks. Even the infants were carrying twigs, whittled to a point. Although it was noon a number of people were also holding pine torches, which sent up greasy black smoke. It was obvious that every single resident of that settlement was determined to have a hand in his death.

Well, thought Sykes, he would just have to try and show them how a Confederate officer could die. That at least would be a novelty for them.

Colonel Sykes was led through a path in the crowd, down to the centre of the hollow. Nobody was sitting nearer than thirty feet to the stake at which he was to be baited and tormented. He noted the eager looks on the faces of those in the ring surrounding the post. They would presumably be getting the first go at jabbing and burning him.

Coils of ropes spun from dried vines lay on the ground and his two attendants worked carefully to secure Sykes's arms to his sides. They tied a rope around his waist, then secured his wrists to it. His legs were left free; he could run as much as he pleased. Having tested the ropes to confirm that he would not be able to work one of his hands free, the men looped a stout rope through the band around his

94

waist, and this they secured to the post. At each stage of their work they tugged hard on the knots, making quite certain that nothing would give. The rope holding him to the stake looked to Colonel Sykes to be about fifty feet in length. When the two young men had finished their preparations they bowed slightly to Sykes and withdrew.

He had never felt so alone in all his life. The colonel stood there, surrounded by men, women and children who had gathered for no other purpose than to see him done to death in the most brutal fashion possible. It occurred to Colonel Sykes that this must be how those men he had seen hanged a few days previously must have felt as they stood on the scaffold, awaiting their hanging. He turned his head to survey the crowd, then turned in a complete circle, wondering when the ferocious assault against him would begin.

From the slopes above came the sound of a woman's scream. Perhaps there was some compassion here for him after all. Not that this would be likely to affect the eventual outcome, but it was heartening to know that at least one person was opposed to his execution. From the direction from which the scream had come there was the sound of raised voices, as though some kind of hubbub was developing. Heads were turning to see what was the case. It might be thought that the colonel would have been grateful for any delay, but truth to tell he would have sooner got the whole dreadful thing over with. The sooner they began, the sooner it would be ended. He was never one for lingering when some unpleasant duty lay before him.

The argument or whatever it was went on and the spectators began to grow restless. Then the voices died down and there was silence again. Sykes braced himself for the horror but, to his astonishment and wonder, the men who had tied him to the post now reappeared, stepping towards him in that same measured tread. When they reached the colonel they drew their knives from the decorated sheaths at their belts and slashed through his bonds. Then they gestured that he was to follow them. The crowd, as baffled as he as to what was going on, parted silently before him as he walked up the slope towards the edge of the natural amphitheatre.

Sitting cross-legged at the top of the slope was a Comanche chief. Next to him was a young woman who stared anxiously at the colonel. It was all most perplexing, until he suddenly realized with a shock that he knew her. She was the girl he had rescued from those scoundrels who had been intent upon raping her. Well, thought Sykes, talk about casting your bread upon the waters!

The chief indicated that Colonel Sykes should sit opposite him, which he did. Then the Indian said, in very passable but accented English, 'My daughter says that you are the man who saved her life.'

'Well, sir, I won't deny that she had her tail in a crack when last I saw her.'

'Were you not afraid to die?'

'When? Then or now?'

The Comanche looked closely at the colonel and then said, 'You are very dark for a white man. Have you Indian blood?'

'It could be so. Leastways, my mother was Spanish and very dark. Lord knows about her forebears. Why?'

'You faced death as one of my own warriors would wish to do. I watched you there at the stake. You looked around with interest, but there was no fear.'

'Would you mind,' said Sykes, 'telling me what now is to become of me? Is this a reprieve or are you no longer resolved to have my blood?'

'You think that I would have killed the man who saved my only daughter?'

'Pardon me, sir, I know little of your ways.'

The chief stood up and addressed the crowd. After he had finished speaking everybody rose and went back to the village. There was a hum of quiet conversation, but whether they were grumbling about missing out on the big show Sykes could not tell.

The Comanche leader said to Sykes, 'Come with me.' He followed the man and the woman at his side to a tepee that was more richly decorated than the others. Every so often, as they walked back to the tents, the young Indian woman cast backward glances at Colonel Sykes, until he began to grow a little uncomfortable.

When they reached the chief's tepee, he turned to his daughter and said a few words. She went off, but not before looking back once more at the colonel.

The chief held open the door flap so that Sykes could enter first.

The interior of the tepee was cool and dark, but there was enough light entering from the hole in the roof for him not to need to strain his eyes to see what was what. When they were inside the Indian lifted off the strange arrangement of feathers that had been perched upon his head.

He said, 'This is my crown. My people like to see me wear it.'

'Are your folk annoyed at losing their day's sport? I dare say they were looking forward to tearing me limb from limb.'

'You think us savages?' asked the chief, as he sat on the animal skins that carpeted the floor of the tent. 'One man is killed like that, once each year. How many men were killed in your war?' He waved his hand towards a hide, which Sykes took as an invitation to sit himself down.

'You have a point,' said Colonel Sykes. 'Perhaps being that one man gave me a prejudiced view of the case.'

'I know what you did for my daughter. She would have been dishonoured and perhaps killed, had you not come along.'

'I would have done the same for any woman in a fix, I do assure you. Glad I could be of service.'

'You know much of our customs, Mister. . . ? I find that I do not know your name. I am called Nacoma. The name means "one who wanders".'

'Thomas Abernethy Sykes, sometime colonel in

the army of the Confederate States of America, at your service.'

'Ah, a soldier. I should have known. We were talking of our customs, I think. You do not know what happens with us when a man rescues somebody from death?'

Colonel Sykes fidgeted and began to grow embarrassed. 'It really is nothing; pray don't mention it again. I am only glad that I was able to be of service.'

'Ah,' said Nacoma. 'You think that the matter ended that day? Not so. Because you saved the girl from death, you and she are bound together for all time. You have a bond which is at least as close as that which she has with her own family.'

Sykes found that he was grateful for the darkness within the tepee, for he felt himself flushing a little at Nacoma's words.

'I'm sure she has no occasion to feel that way,' he muttered. 'This is deuced awkward, sir, if you don't mind my saying so. I would be pleased if you were to forget the whole thing, really.'

Nacoma watched Colonel Sykes, his face immobile. It was not possible to say whether he was amused or offended by what the colonel was saying. The tepee was suddenly flooded with light as the door flap was pulled aside and the young woman under discussion entered, bearing a tray of food and gourds of drink. She smiled slightly at the colonel, who nodded politely to her. Instead of leaving at once she began to talk to her father in an animated and excited manner. For his part Nacoma merely nodded or shook his head slightly. When his daughter had finished speaking he reached out his hand and spoke a few words to her. She glanced once more at the colonel and left the tent.

I wonder what the devil all that was about? thought Colonel Sykes. There is more to the case here than I am knowing and it puts me in a tricky position. I can't afford to offend the chief and yet all this talk about his daughter looks to me as though it is tending in a very strange direction. I suppose I'll have to see how the cards are dealt.

The two men ate and drank without speaking. When they had finished Nacoma produced a pipe and filled it with tobacco. Then he lit it and smoked for a few seconds before handing the pipe to Sykes. They smoked companionably in this way for ten minutes, neither of them saying anything.

At last the chief said, to Colonel Sykes's utter astonishment, 'My daughter tells me that she wishes to marry you.'

This was bad enough, putting the colonel in what was a very delicate position indeed, but worse was to follow when the chief added as an afterthought, 'It is time she took a husband. She is fifteen.'

Sykes almost choked at this new intelligence. Fifteen! He could imagine few things more indecent than the idea of a man of his age being hitched up to a child of fifteen. Determined as he was to conceal his feelings from the man before him, who had the power of life and death over the colonel, Sykes could not help letting out a slight and involuntary gasp

100

when he learned of the girl's true age.

Nacoma misinterpreted this and said proudly, 'You think that my daughter would not be a fit wife for you? Perhaps you see us as you did your black slaves, more like beasts than real people.'

Despite his fixed intention to avoid offending or falling out with the Comanche chief, Colonel Sykes could not restrain himself at this.

He said stiffly, 'I do not recall that the Confederate army harried you from your own land, as the forces of the United States are now doing. We left you and your people alone and allowed you to live as you wished, according to your old ways.'

Nacoma said nothing for a space and then admitted, 'This is true.'

It was, thought Sykes, a time for blunt words.

'Nacoma,' he said, 'may I speak plainly? We are two men and need not fence with each other. I will tell you my thoughts on this and you may judge me as you wish.'

This was the best possible line that the colonel could have adopted with this wily old chief.

Nacoma said simply, 'Speak.'

'There are two strong objections against a match between me and your daughter. The one is general and the other very specific. I grew up in the South and saw a number of matches between white men and black women, white women and Indians and every combination you could ever dream of. None of them ever worked out well. All those sorts of things, where men from one world married into women

101

from another, every one of them went bad. To me there is the river and the land. Both are well enough in their own way and one is not better than the other. But where the river and the land meet there is mud, slime and a stink.'

There was no sign as to whether the chief agreed with Colonel Sykes or had been mortally offended by his views on interracial marriage. He merely said, 'What is your other reason?'

'I have made a promise to help somebody. Until that oath has been fulfilled, I am not a free man.'

'An oath? Tell me about it.'

Sykes found himself relating to Nacoma the details of his recent history, including his time in the condemned cell and the strange circumstances that led to his being granted his freedom. Then he told him how it had chanced that he rescued the chief's daughter. Nacoma was a good listener and did not interrupt, except to ask one or two pertinent questions.

When the colonel had finished his tale, Nacoma said, 'That is the strangest story I have heard for many a year. Your life has become like one of our legends, Colonel. It is a thousand pities that you are not free to take my daughter to wife, but there it is. You have said yourself, you cannot rest until you have carried out this task. But what a husband you would have made, all the same! You are a great warrior.'

Sykes shrugged. 'I'm no great shakes on the warrior front, Nacoma. The fact that I fetched up here should be enough proof of that.'

The Comanche rose. 'Would you like to see my people? Not as their victim, but as a respected guest?'

'I would be honoured, sir.'

It did not escape Colonel Sykes's notice that he was the object of great and avid curiosity as he strolled through the Comanche settlement with their chief. An hour earlier and they would cheerfully have tortured him to death; now, the women and children smiled at him and even the men nodded politely as he passed. It really was a remarkable reversal of fortune.

As he walked through the lanes that separated the lines of tepees Sykes could not help but wonder why on earth the army could not just leave these people in peace. They were nomads, moving from place to place, living by hunting. In general, they harmed nobody and there was no good reason that he could see to 'concentrate' them in one location, as the plans for their future entailed. He asked Nacoma about this and the chief proved to have a sharper political insight than Sykes was himself possessed of.

The Comanche said, 'Those men in Washington cannot put up with other nations. They want to rule everywhere; one nation, with them in charge. That's why they crushed your Confederacy. Free Indians offend them. They want to make sure we follow the same laws as their own people. Live like them, obey them. They are the enemies of freedom.'

'Amen to that,' said Sykes. 'I reckon that you have reasoned out the case just right, sir. It was that which irked them about us in the South. We were happy to

103

belong to their Union, but wanted to live life in our own way and that's what got their goat.'

After they had walked through the whole village Nacoma led the colonel back to his tepee. When they were seated within he said to Sykes, 'We have all your war gear, Colonel. I hope that you will accept, as a gift, a weapon of our own.' He handed Colonel Sykes a beautifully decorated sheath, within which was an enormous and razor-sharp knife, not unlike a version of the Bowie knife.

'You and your people are not my enemies,' said Colonel Sykes sincerely. 'Were it left to me, I would be happy for you people to carry on roaming as you do now. I am afeared, though, that your days are numbered for that. You know that the cavalry will be riding down on you any day now to force you from your land.'

'We shall see what will arrive to us. There is no purpose in meeting trouble halfway,' said the chief. 'I will explain to my daughter how things stand. Will you speak to her before you leave us?'

'It would be my pleasure,' said the colonel. 'By the by, what is her name?'

'She is called Naduah, the one who moves gracefully.'

CHAPTER 8

Now that he had been told her actual age, Colonel Sykes could see how young the Indian girl called Naduah really was. Why, she was only a child! Nacoma had told him that the girl spoke very little English and, since Sykes's command of the Comanche language was nothing remarkable, he supposed that he would just have to explain as best he could and hope that she made some sense of it all.

The colonel and the young girl were walking near to the village and he had the uncomfortable feeling that the two of them were the subject of pretty lively interest among those in the Comanche settlement.

He stopped walking and said to the girl, 'Naduah, I don't know how much of this you will understand, but I have to tell you that I am not free to marry. I have a hard task to undertake, fighting and such. I don't know if I will come out of it alive on the other side and it wouldn't be fair to you to let you tie your-self to me. Given the circumstances, I mean.'

Naduah spoke a few words to him, looking straight

into his eyes.

He said, 'I'm right sorry, child, but I cannot make sense of what you are saying. I'm pleased that I was able to do you a service, and if I pass through this way again I will make sure to look you out.'

The girl spoke again and looked so plaintive and sad that the colonel could not maintain his formal air. He held out his arms and embraced her, kissing her chastely on the forehead. Then he stepped back and spoke again, with a smile playing around the corners of his mouth.

'I will not say how I might have greeted your proposal, had I been twenty years younger. You are a fine girl and I hope that you will find a good man to be your husband.'

From a bag that hung around her waist the Indian girl drew a headband, woven of tiny beads and decorated with feathers. She held it out for Sykes. Lord, he thought, I hope that I am not compromising myself by accepting such a gift. For aught I know to the contrary, this might have the significance of an offer of betrothal.

Notwithstanding, he took the headband and admired it, saying, 'I reckon you made this with your own hands, Naduah, or I miss my guess. Thank you. Thank you very much.' He set it around his head, wondering what sort of fool he looked like. In fact, it suited him well enough, giving him a raffish and exotic look. At any rate, the girl was pleased, clapping her hands in delight at the sight of him wearing her favour.

When he took his leave of the Comanche chief, Sykes said, 'You have a fine daughter there, sir, if I'm any judge. I hope she marries well.'

'Remember, though, what I told you,' said Nacoma. 'Whatever else happens, you and she are linked together. You are as much kin to her now as I am.'

'I shall not forget,' said the colonel gravely, although privately thinking to himself that he should think twice before rescuing another girl in that way. He had had no idea that he was forging a lifelong bond by his simple action.

As he rode off from the village he thought to himself, I hope that President Johnson does not adopt the same line if I succeed in saving that niece of his. Being kin to Andrew Johnson would not be half as agreeable as being connected with Nacoma.

The chief had shown him the direction to Fort Bennett and the first thought that came to Sykes's head was that he would be best advised not to ride right up to the front gates. He decided to ride round in a wide circle, which would ultimately bring him in from the opposite direction to the Comanche village. It would mean riding for the rest of the day and then sleeping out again, but he didn't think that Don Jose would be be leaving for another few days.

Nacoma had sent him off with all the equipment with which he had arrived, as well as the knife and its elaborately decorated sheath. Combined with the headband, it made Colonel Sykes look somewhat outlandish. It was early evening when he set out and

107

his intention was to ride on steadily until darkness fell and then camp up for the night. He calculated that he was presently about ten miles from Fort Bennett and, on his current path, was not getting any closer as he rode. It was probably far enough away for him not to be unduly worried about bumping into any of Don Jose's men.

The plateau of Cejita de los Comancheros was to his right as the colonel rode along and the rise of land leading to it curved away, so that he could not see more than half a mile ahead of him. In this way, he carried on for a couple of hours, until the darkening sky told him that it would soon be time to settle down for the night.

The shot took Colonel Sykes altogether by surprise. One minute he had been trotting gently along, minding his own business and keeping an eye out for a likely spot to shelter for the night, and the next a musket ball was buzzing angrily past his head. He reined in and raised his hands above his head. Having no idea at all who had shot at him, to say nothing of how many people were involved, it would have been foolhardy in the extreme to begin a firefight in the twilight. After all, whoever had fired that shot could obviously see *him*, even if he could not see the unknown assailant. He thought it entirely possible that somebody had drawn down on him at this very second; going for his gun would be inviting another bullet. Besides, that first shot had probably been in the nature of a warning, rather than an attempt to end his life. Otherwise, why had there been no more shooting?

The colonel's instincts were proved right a few seconds later, when somebody up in the rocks to his right called down, 'You stay right where you are, pilgrim. Go for your gun or even lower those hands and you are a dead man.' There was nothing to do under the circumstances other than to sit tight and wait to see how things played out.

There was not long to wait before Sykes found out what was afoot. There was a scrambling and cursing, combined with a miniature avalanche of pebbles and stones, as two men made their way down the slope towards him. To the colonel's amazement they were wearing the uniform of the US Cavalry.

'What we got here?' asked one of the men in a jocular tone. 'Looks like some half-breed to me.'

'Half-breed be damned to you,' said Colonel Sykes irritably. 'Half-breed yourself!'

'Don't see that many white men wearing wampum beads round they heads,' said the man. 'What say, Carter?'

His colleague agreed, remarking, 'He's dark enough too. I'd say a 'breed for sure.'

'When you two vagabonds have finished speculating upon my ancestry,' said the colonel, thoroughly annoyed by now, 'you might care to glance in a looking-glass yourselves. Judging by the look of the pair of you, your own mothers and fathers were probably scarecrows.'

'You watch your mouth, mister,' advised one of the troopers. 'Keep a civil tongue in your head and there might not be the need for any more gunplay. Now, answer straight: who are you and what are you doing in these parts?'

Sykes lowered his hands very slowly, taking great care that he did not give the impression that he was going for a gun. Then he said, 'I don't know that you fellows have any more authority here than I have myself. You are not peace officers, nor anything like.'

'Oh, Carter, see what we got here?' said one of them mockingly. 'Some kind of judge advocate or something of that brand.' He turned to Sykes and said in an ugly voice, 'Regular expert on the law, ain't you? Well, let me tell you now that this whole area has been interdicted, if you know what that means.'

'I know what it means well enough,' said Colonel Sykes, 'but I don't see that it concerns me overmuch. I am not smuggling goods or carrying anything unlawful from one place to another.'

'Ain't you, though? What about that pistol in your belt or that rifle back there? You say you ain't moving them around?'

'You can't be telling me that it is unlawful to carry firearms out here? I never heard the like. Where are your officers?'

'Don't you fret none about that. We're taking you to meet our captain right now and see what he wants to do with you. You'll find we got pretty wide powers since the order was signed yesterday.'

'Order?' said Sykes sharply. 'What order?'

The man seemed pleased at the consternation that his words had caused the colonel, because he smiled and said triumphantly, 'Why, the order placing this whole damned territory under martial law. You didn't hear about it? Too bad for you. The army has powers you never even dreamed of.'

It was on the very tip of Sykes's tongue to say, *Including the power to set baboons like you two up to pester decent folk,* but he chose instead to remain silent. Doubtless, he could deal more readily with an officer.

In spite of their words, the troopers did not actually disarm the colonel, perhaps having decided that he might genuinely be a person of note, but they took him round the bluff of rock that had prevented him from seeing the plain ahead. There, stretched out in front of his eyes, was an encampment of cavalry. Neat rows of tents showed that there must be at least fifty men here. Sykes saw, to his utter disbelief, that they even had an artillery piece with them: a twelve-pounder howitzer, unless he was very much mistaken. He turned to the men escorting him and asked, 'What in God's name are you people up to?'

'Less of the questions,' replied one of the soldiers. 'The captain will tell you as much as he sees fit.'

The three of them, Sykes on his horse and the two troopers on foot, approached the centre of the camp, where the colonel found that their captain was none other than Captain Stanton, who had accompanied him all the way from Milledgeville to Camp Edgewood. Stanton greeted him cheerfully. 'Colonel Sykes, good of you to drop by.'

'Do you know this man, sir?' asked one of the troopers.

'Yes, yes, Burton. I can vouch for the colonel. Leave us be now.'

When the others had gone, Stanton said, 'Get down from your horse, Colonel, and allow me to entertain you. Have you had any sort of luck in your quest?'

As he dismounted, Sykes said, 'I know where the girl is and have spoken with her.'

'The devil you have! I thought you would be down at the border looking for her.'

Colonel Sykes laughed. 'No, I never thought to find her that far south. She is only a few miles from here.'

'Is she, by Godfrey? Any chance that we can ride over and collect her?'

'That is apt to prove a little tricky, Captain. Perhaps we can discuss it once I am settled down and have a drink in my hand. If, that is, your camp runs to such luxuries?'

'I think that we might run to a glass of whiskey. I hope you're taking good care of our horse?'

'Do you have any reason to doubt it?'

'No. Let me get somebody to look after it, while we have a little talk.' Captain Stanton called to a passing soldier. 'Hey, you there. Just take the colonel here's horse, will you, and look after it?'

When Sykes was sitting on a camp stool in Stanton's tent with a glass of whiskey in his hand, he said, 'I have an idea that there is more to you than first meets the eye, Captain. When we met a few days ago I understood you to be no more than a glorified messenger boy. Now, I find you commanding this force out here. You said nothing about this when we parted at Camp Edgewood.'

Stanton thought for a few moments before replying. Then he said, 'My role is a little unusual. You might say that I am a troubleshooter for the White House. There have been two serious problems down this way, one of which was trying to find the President's niece. This present enterprise is the second of my assignments in this neck of the woods.'

'You wouldn't, I suppose,' said the colonel, 'care to share with me the details of this other business which occupies you in New Mexico?'

'I'm sorry, Colonel. That is strictly secret.'

'I only thought that if it had any reference to ten Gatling guns, then I might be able to lend a hand.'

'Now, how the hell do you know about that?'

'I have my sources, Captain Stanton. I just want to make sure that we don't get in each other's way, that's all. Tomorrow I hope to free Elizabeth Harper and I don't see how having your company of hotheads fooling around in the near vicinity is going to make the job any easier.'

'I think that we need to talk turkey, Colonel Sykes. Recovering those guns is more important now than the girl. President Johnson comprehends that perfectly. You undertook to rescue Elizabeth Harper in good faith and I will vouch for it that you did your best. But you cannot jeopardize what I am doing.

113

And on another note, have you been visiting the Comanches? That is a strange article of apparel around your head.'

'I haven't been giving secrets to the Indians, if that's what you're asking. And you will forgive me if I don't share your view of the case, Captain. I said that I would free that young woman and free her I will. I just don't want our paths to get tangled, so that we are tripping over each other's feet.'

Captain Stanton poured them both another drink and said, 'How about a little walk? I have to check a few things and we can talk as I make my inspection. Leave the drinks here. I don't want my men to think I have taken to drink.'

As they walked round the camp, Sykes's eyes missed nothing at all. It hardly needed a military genius to see that these men were going to be using their field gun to breach walls and then send in their cavalry. This meant, of course, that Stanton knew where the Gatlings were. The colonel was guiltily aware that the young captain probably didn't know, though, that the guns were now assembled and in working order. Even with their single howitzer, there was every chance of the engagement turning into a massacre. There was nothing for it: he would have to explain the situation. With luck, he and Stanton could join forces and achieve each of their aims at the same time.

As they strolled along the perimeter of the camp Sykes said, 'What is the urgency over the Gatling guns? I thought that the army was giving them to Juàrez.'

Stanton shot him a sharp and suspicious look,

remarking, 'You seem to know all about our deepest secrets, Colonel. I can't help wondering if we didn't perhaps take a wrong turn when we hired you and brought you down here.'

'Don't say that you repent of saving me from the gallows, Captain?' said the colonel, laughing. 'That's hardly gracious of you!'

Captain Stanton couldn't help joining in the laughter as he said, 'No, I am happy enough to have been the instrument of saving your life. I just hope that you are not going to be in the way.'

'I suppose that I should tell you two things at once, although neither will be pleasing to you. Well, that is three things in total. In the first instance, I know that you have it in mind to mount an assualt on Fort Bennett.'

'That is so, yes. Although how you could know about it is more than I can say. This is supposed to be a top-secret, eyes-only operation, and here is a Confederate officer who knows all about it. How do you do it?'

'That doesn't signify. The next thing you must know is that Elizabeth Harper is in Fort Bennett this minute. She isn't a prisoner, though. She is canoodling with Don Jose, the leader of that band of desperadoes.'

'How come? I thought that she'd been snatched by the Comanche.'

'That's nothing to the purpose. But things are about to change. I think that she might yet end up as a hostage.'

'What is the final piece of information that you think I ought to be apprised of, Colonel Sykes?'

'It is this, and I will freely admit my own role in the matter: all ten of those Gatling guns are now in working order and probably loaded to boot. Your men will be cut to pieces if you ride against those comancheros.'

This news was not received well. Captain Stanton stopped dead in his tracks and turned to face the older man.

'I do not believe for one single moment that that crew of ragamuffins could have assembled those weapons without external assistance. Please assure me that you played no part in this, Colonel Sykes?'

'Can't be done. It was I who put them together and showed Don Jose's men how to work them.'

There was an awkward silence before the captain spoke again. When he did, the words sounded as though they had been chipped from ice.

'You may or may not know, Colonel Sykes, that this part of New Mexico is now under martial law. I could bring you before a drumhead court martial and have you shot for this. Don't think that I would not.'

The ghost of an exceedingly bleak smile flitted briefly across the colonel's lips. He said, 'That would make the third time in a week that I lay under sentence of death from three different authorities. If I were a superstitious man, I might think that it was my destiny to be done to death by enemies.'

Glimpsing the smile and taking it amiss, Captain Stanton said harshly, 'This is no laughing matter. I am more than half-minded to have you clapped in irons this very minute.'

'Will you at least allow me to explain my actions; before you take any hasty and precipitate action, that is?'

'I will. But I tell you now that this explanation of yours had best be a very good one. From where I stand right now, you have the appearance of a man who is playing some crooked game of his own and setting one group of us against the others. You have not told me yet what you were doing playing kiss-in-the-ring with the Comanches. I mean it, Colonel. If I find that you are up to something that tends to work against my interests, I shall not hesitate to crush you.'

'You have me all wrong. I was given a job to do, by you yourself, and all that I have been doing since we parted is endeavouring to undertake that commission to the best of my ability.'

Captain Stanton stared hard at Sykes for a good thirty seconds, then said, 'Come back to my tent now and tell me precisely what you have been up to. Do not fox with me or hold anything back. I am a mighty suspicious person, Colonel, and I do not altogether trust you right now.'

CHAPTER 9

Back at the captain's tent the two men sat down on camp stools, facing each other and with their drinks in their hands. The atmosphere was cool, but by no means as frosty as it had been. Stanton was prepared to hear the colonel's side of the matter.

Sykes said, 'I found Miss Harper by offering my services to Don Jose and his band. I had no idea that it related to those damned Gatling guns of yours. Since the story I heard was that you people had made a gift of them to Juàrez, I saw no harm in getting them in order before they were transported to Mexico. There, I don't think that you can criticize my actions. Tell me, what is all this fuss now about the things? If they were being given to the rebels in any case, why should it matter whether they were in pieces or ready for action?'

'You already appear to know most of the business, so I suppose there is no harm in filling in those few gaps in your knowledge. Mind, I look to you to keep this to yourself. Fact is, sending heavy weaponry to

Juàrez and his men is not and has never been official government policy. We've been leaving them muskets, powder and shot, but it recently came to light that some damn-fool politician has been teaming up with somebody in the War Office to transport more than that. We found out about the Gatlings too late to stop their being dispatched south. There was even talk about supplying the rebels with field guns, if you don't mind.'

Sykes thought about it for a while, then said, 'I can't see the nature of the problem. You're arming the rebels anyway. What odds does it make if you give them heavier weapons? You want them to win, don't you?'

'Of course we want them to win. We want it to look as though they drove out the French and deposed the emperor by their own efforts, though. It does not suit us to have it look like the United States is meddling in the internal affairs of a neighbouring country. They could have acquired muskets anywhere, but if they take to the field backed by Gatlings and field artillery, then it will look to all the world as though we have been involved. It must look like an all-Mexican effort. We don't wish to fall out with the European powers.'

At this, Colonel Sykes threw back his head and roared with laughter.

'Why, I never heard such hypocrisy in my life. You mean you are happy to overthrow the government of Mexico, but only if you can guy it up to look as though you didn't have a hand in it?'

119

'You needn't laugh,' said Stanton tetchily. 'If ten brand-new Gatling guns show up in rebel hands it will be plain as a pikestaff that they were from the USA. It would be an embarrassment. I have to get them back before they get anywhere near the border.'

'Where do the Indians fit into your scheme?'

'Indians? The Indians have no part in this. If they do not interfere, then I have no interest in them. This is a small force. The aim is to make a lightning raid on that fort, seize back the Gatlings and take them to Camp Edgewood.'

'You cannot launch an attack on Fort Bennett while that girl is there,' said Sykes firmly. 'Like as not, she would be killed in the crossfire. You must hold off until I have had a chance to get her out of there.'

'I told you, Colonel. The Gatlings are now more important than the President's niece. We are at risk of a grave diplomatic incident. The girl will have to take her chance. You say that she is there voluntarily; well then, she is the architect of her own misfortune.'

'You do not know me at all. If you think that I will stand by while a helpless young woman is killed because of some foolish squabble in Washington, then you are plumb mistaken. I said that I would rescue that girl and so I will. What time are you planning to attack the fort?'

'That's classified information, Colonel.'

'All right. You do not want to start your assault in broad daylight. Not now you know that they have ten Gatlings ready for action. You only have, what, fifty men at your command? You couldn't do it.'

'What is your proposal?'

'Delay your attack until night has fallen. Use your field gun and you can batter the place into submission without hazarding your men. You can bring the piece up under the cover of darkness. Those Gatlings will be no use in pitch dark against men they cannot even see.'

'There's some merit in your plan, I will allow. How will you get the girl out before we begin our bombardment? If, that is, I go along with your ideas.'

'Leave that to me. Can you let me have a coil of rope from your stores?'

'I dare say. You surely do not have it in mind to enter that fortress by stealth?'

'When I say I'll do a thing, Captain Stanton, then I'll do it or die in the attempt. When a helpless girl is also involved, then I will do anything needful. I said I'd rescue that young woman and so I will.'

Spending the evening in Stanton's camp was certainly a more agreeable way to pass the time than camping up alone in some little canyon would have been. The two officers had reached a modus vivendi and it had been agreed that the captain would not commence firing on Fort Bennett until two hours after the sun had set. This was cutting it extremely fine from Sykes's point of view, but it was as far as Captain Stanton was prepared to go in delaying his own plans. It would mean that the colonel would have only an hour at most, when once he had got into the fort, to find Elizabeth Harper and persuade her to leave at once.

One of the things that his comrades had observed about Sykes was that he was always at his best when his back was to the wall. It was under those circumstances that his brain worked most rapidly and to greatest effect. Danger of death acted on him like some stimulant, causing him to come to life in a way that ordinary and humdrum existence did not. It was this that he found so dreadful about running the farm after the war had ended. When he had returned there after the surrender his overseer had gone and all the slaves had made off, taking with them anything of value from the big house.

For nearly a year Sykes had run the old farm single handed: ploughing and planting, reaping and repairing, tending to everything about the house and land that needed doing. It wasn't that it couldn't be done; it was manifestly possible for one man to keep the farm ticking over, although obviously upon a much smaller scale than before. The question was, why? Why would a man spend his life working so, with nothing to look forward to other than his bed at night?

Looking back on that year of heavy toil, it seemed now to Colonel Sykes to be a like a dream, and a pretty disagreeable dream at that. It would be overstating the case grossly to call it a nightmare, but it was no way for a man such as he to live. There was no zest in such a life, nothing to excite one or set the blood pounding through the veins.

After spending the better part of a year like that, the colonel knew that something would have to give. His involvement in the execution of the Yankee soldier had provided a neat full stop to his career in agriculture. After the adventures of the last few days, he knew for certain sure that he would not be going back to raise crops for a second year. Let his brother take over the old place and try his hand at farming. He, Colonel Thomas Sykes, was finished with that particular line of work.

Stanton introduced the colonel to some of his men and although they were a little taken aback to find a former senior officer in the Confederate army moving about freely in the middle of a most secret military operation, they thought that if the captain was happy about it then it was not for them to raise any objection.

As they walked through the camp Stanton said suddenly, 'I could not help but notice that you have been knocked about a bit since last we met. Will you be up to the sort of lively games needed tomorrow? Forgive me for asking, but our plans do hinge upon each other, in a sense.'

'I was beaten by some cowardly rascals while I was trussed up like a chicken. There's no harm done, bar a cracked rib or two.'

'So you weren't able to give as good as you got?'

'I was not. But there's a reckoning to be paid there and, with good fortune, I should be able to settle that account tomorrow night as well.'

After they had toured the camp and been social with the men, Captain Stanton suggested that he and Sykes might enjoy one last glass of bourbon before turning in for the night. Nothing loath, the colonel agreed at once and the two of them retired to Stanton's quarters for a final drink.

'At what hour will you set out tomorrow?' asked Stanton.

'I am hoping to sweep right round Fort Bennett and approach it from the rear. I reackon that there will not be any sentries facing backward.'

'How's that?'

'It is the position of the fort,' explained Sykes. 'It is facing the plain and it guards the way up to the plateau. Behind it lies Cejita de los Comancheros. It is not in reason that they should be expecting any enemy to come from that direction. No, they will be watching to the front. Remember that they are hoping to leave the fort for good in a very few days.'

'Do you feel able to share with me your intentions?'

'It's simple enough. I shall gain access to the fort and then speak to Elizabeth Harper. If she is agreeable, then I will take her to safety before you begin your attack.'

'It sounds easy when you say it quickly like that,' said Captain Stanton. 'Tell me really, how do you rate your chances? You are not throwing your life away for what you see as a matter of honour?'

'If a man were to throw his life away, I can think of no better cause than what you are pleased to term, "a

124

matter of honour". But no, I don't believe that I am about to lose my life in this venture, although one never knows for sure.'

'Well, I hope that we both achieve our ends tomorrow night, Colonel Sykes. You have played the part for which you were engaged and I do not think that any man could have done better.'

'You flatter me, Captain Stanton. I shall have played my part, as you put it, when that young woman is safely restored to her family. Until that time, I have failed miserably.'

The morning dawned bleak and grey, with a threat of rain from the hills above the camp. This did not entirely displease Stanton, because, as he remarked to Colonel Sykes, a nice thunderstorm would drive men to shelter and make them less likely to be standing on the ramparts, peering out inquisitively into the night.

'Is there aught else we can furnish you with?' asked Stanton.

'I don't think so,' said Colonel Sykes thoughtfully. 'I have a rifle and pistol, five pounds of fine-grained powder and the knife which that Comanche chief was kind enough to give me. And of course the rope that you yourself provided. No, I will do well enough, I believe.'

'Do you have a watch?' asked Captain Stanton.

'Why, yes.' Sykes pulled out a massive and old-fashioned pocket watch. 'Why do you ask?'

'I wish to make sure that we are both working to

the same timetable. Here now, let us set both our watches together.'

They did so, fiddling with the hands until the two timepieces were running within a few seconds of each other.

'Recollect now,' said the captain, 'I shall open fire with our howitzer promptly at ten tonight. I aim to fire canister shot into that pest-hole as fast as my gunners are able and then to shoot at any men who emerge. There will be no call for surrender; the first those boys will know of it is when the shells start flying.'

'I suppose that this is the modern way of warfare. It seems a cowardly way to proceed. You might at the very least give them a chance to give up their ordnance without a fight.'

'Yes, that's likely, isn't it?' said Stanton sarcastically. 'With ten Gatling guns ranged against us? No, stopping those guns going south is my only priority. Just make sure you and the girl are clear of the fort by ten.'

Sykes chafed at the hanging around, but it would serve no useful purpose to turn up at Fort Bennett before darkness had fallen. He walked around, chatting in a desultory way with the troopers, most of whom were intrigued to know what the connection was between their captain and the former enemy officer. They tried in vain to pump Colonel Sykes, then, finding that this was useless, fell to talking idly with him of this and that.

By midday the colonel had had enough and was

keen to be on his way. After sharing the same rations as the men, he told Stanton that he was leaving.

'Just as you like,' said the captain. 'I should feel the same in your place. What will you do, work your way round to the higher ground and see what can be seen?'

'Yes, I think so. The slope grows a little steeper behind the fort and I don't think that I will be seen, provided that I keep a mile or so from it. I should be able to use these field glasses to good effect from that distance and glean some notion of how things are going.'

'Well, take care.' Stanton put out his hand and Colonel Sykes gripped it warmly. 'Mind now, Colonel, be clear of the fort by ten.'

It felt good to be free of the cavalry encampment. The war had only ended a year since and it still felt odd to be walking at his ease in the midst of Union soldiers. They all struck Sykes as decent enough fellows, but really, their aims and his did not precisely coincide. For his part, he could hardly care less about the Gatling guns and felt privately that Stanton was making a lot of fuss about nothing. Not that it was any affair of his, of course.

There was a narrow track curling north-east, up towards the plateau, and along this Sykes took his horse at a walk. There surely was no sort of hurry and he could not even think of entering the fort for another eight hours or more. Overhead, birds of prey wheeled across the cloudy grey sky, while below him, on the plain, he could see Stanton's men breaking camp and preparing for battle stations.

Captain Stanton was an interesting fellow. There was still a lot more to him than Sykes could figure, but the important point was that he came across to the colonel as being a trustworthy and honest man.

Slowly, the colonel made his way on to the high plains which bordered Colorado and Texas. The air was sharp and clear up here and there was not a single sign of Man and his works. It was a good place for being alone with your thoughts.

As he rode Sykes kept a sharp eye out for mischief. This area of the high plains was regarded by the comancheros as their own exclusive territory and they did not welcome strangers overmuch. He saw nobody, though, for the next three hours.

When he was fairly sure that he must be above Fort Bennett and roughly to the north of it, the colonel dismounted and began heading due south, where the land sloped into a series of terraces. Just as he had expected, the fort lay a mile or so to the south.

As soon as he caught sight of it Sykes led the horse back a little and then let her graze on the sparse grass that covered the soil on this rocky shelf. Having done so, the colonel crawled on his hands and knees, back towards the fort, making sure that he did not present a silhouette or profile that could be seen from below. Then he settled down with the field glasses and surveyed the land below him.

They were a good pair of glasses. Colonel Sykes could see right down into the compound and even recognize individual people. One of the first to catch his eye was Elizabeth Harper. She was still roaming free, so it must be assumed that she did not yet know that Don Jose was planning to drop her before they reached Mexico. At any rate, her status must still be that of favoured pet and not hostage to be ransomed. In the latter case, they would scarcely let her walk about freely like that.

Having satisfied himself that his target was safely in place and readily accessible, Sykes turned his attention to the rear wall of the fort. It was constructed chiefly of adobe, but was probably strengthened within by wooden beams. That would account for the stubs of tree trunks that protruded from the external walls at a height of ten or twelve feet. It should not prove too arduous to cast a noose around one of those and thus climb on to the parapet.

Mind, a lot would depend upon luck. There was an internal walkway all round the walls, but the colonel could see no earthly reason for Don Jose to post sentries looking in this direction. Any threat would be coming from the lower ground to the south-west.

Having satisfied himself that the fort's defences were as he recalled, Sykes put away the field glasses. He had been shielding the lenses to protect against the possibility of glints of reflected sunlight, but he didn't feel like taking unnecessary chances. The sun had broken through the clouds and all it needed now was for one of those men to see a flash from up here and it would all be up with him. He might as well signal them with a heliograph!

Colonel Sykes wriggled back to where he had left the marc munching disconsolately on the prickly weeds and undernourished grass to be found up here. He settled himself with his back resting against a boulder and thought through his plan of battle. One thing was crystal-clear to him: it was that he need not waste any sympathy on those wretches down there in the fort. They made their living, one way or another, through buying and selling human misery. Rifles to the Indians, traded for captives to be ransomed or sold; it was a filthy business, of that there was no doubt.

Having established to his own satisfaction that he was embarked upon a right course of action, Sykes mused about the future. No harm would befall the farm if it were left alone for a few months. He knew that his younger brother would be only too happy to move his family in there if Sykes gave him the nod. Even with the war raging in Mexico, there would surely be the possibility of sending a message from a border town such as El Paso. The colonel had more or less decided to make his way across the border there, to do as Hunter had suggested and seek a commission with Juàrez. If, as everybody thought was the case, Juàrez was to become the next leader of Mexico, then those who had fought beside him would be well placed for advancement.

It did not strike Sykes as a bad idea to take one last look at the approach to Fort Bennett from the rear, just to see if there were any slight angle or advantage that he might so far have neglected. So it proved to be, because this time, while he was looking down, he saw something which had not caught his eye before. It was a dried-up riverbed, running a hundred yards or so behind the back wall of the fort.

Colonel Sykes traced this as far as he could, finding that it wound its way round the slope above Fort Bennett. If he could lead the horse down and get into that watercourse he would be able to get right up close to the wall in which he was interested. It might be a trick of perspective, but from where he was situated here, the riverbed looked to him to be ten feet or so deep; more like a little chasm than anything else.

When the sun was completely below the horizon and twilight was beginning to blanket the high plains, Colonel Sykes checked his equipment one last time and began leading his horse down towards the dry river course that he had spotted. True, he had no reason to think that anybody would be watching out for him, but an ounce of extra precaution never did any harm. The mare was happy to plod along slowly, stopping at intervals to investigate any succulent sprouts of weed that caught her attention.

For his own part, Sykes was in no hurry at all. If the girl was ready to jump ship and come with him it would be a rushed business. He didn't look to be having any long and complicated conversations when once he had gained entrance to the fort.

All of which only went to show that while Colonel Thomas Sykes might well have been a whale of a

131

fellow at military theory and practice, he was a
hopeless dud when it came to judging women and
their ways.

CHAPTER 10

The riverbed could not have been better suited to his purposes had it been dug for him by a company of engineers. Colonel Sykes was able to walk along next to the horse with as little care as if he was looking round his own estate. Every so often he scambled up the side of the bank to peep at the fort. Just as he had gauged, he was able to get within a hundred yards of the back wall of Fort Bennett without any subterfuge or need for concealment.

When he was as close to the fort as it was possible to be Sykes halted and looked round for a convenient place to tether the mare. A tree stump leaned from the bank at a crazy angle, so he tied her bridle to this and said, 'I'll be back soon, don't be afeared.'

He then removed his pack and rooted around, deciding what to take with him. The rifle was too unwieldy to climb with and any fighting was most likely to be close-quarters work. In the end he left it propped against a rock. The Colt Army he had tucked handily into his belt. At his hip, threaded through that same belt, was the knife given to him by Nacoma, and the coil of rope scrounged from Stanton's stores was slung over his shoulder.

The colonel looked over the contents of his pack and then, on the spur of the moment, picked up the keg of powder and length of fuse, saying as he did so, 'Sykes, my boy, you never know when some powder will come in handy and that's a fact!'

Sykes cut a length off the coil of rope with the Comanche knife and fashioned a makeshift sling for the little keg of powder, so that it would hang easily over his shoulder. Then he climbed up the riverbank and went loping to the wall of the fort.

Scaling the wall did not look to be an arduous task. It would simply be a question of securing the rope to one of the wooden beams jutting out near the top of the wall. Colonel Sykes tied a noose in the end of the rope and threw it up and over one of the pieces of wood. He wasn't trying to lasso the thing; his skills were not too well developed in that way, but rather so that the rope just caught over the beam. He managed this at the third attempt. He paid the rope out, letting the weight of the noose bring it towards him. Then he simply pulled one end of the rope through the noose, pulled it tight and the rope was neatly secured to the beam.

Climbing up the rope was harder than Sykes had bargained for; the cracked ribs were hurting damnably and at one point he thought that he might pass out with the pain, as he took all the strain of his weight on his arms. He gained the wooden posts in the end and then rested for a moment before standing up and scrambling over the parapet. He almost landed right in the lap of the young man who was crouched there having a quiet smoke. This young fellow did not know at all what to make of a man appearing from nowhere in this way and he jumped up, spooked by the colonel's sudden arrival.

Before he could speak, let alone cry out for help, Sykes had drawn the fearsome blade that Nacoma had given him at their parting and slashed it with all his strength across the man's throat. The blood sprayed out from the severed artery and, almost by reflex, Colonel Sykes pitched the fellow over the low wall, so that nobody would stumble across his body. All this had taken only a few seconds.

There was nobody in sight below. Judging from the sounds of gaiety coming from the main gate, some sort of festivity was going on, which meant that, with a little luck, Sykes might have the run of the place as long as he was careful.

After a moment's thought the colonel decided to leave the rope where it was, hanging from the beam. It was exceedingly unlikely that anybody would be walking round outside that wall in the dark, and having the thing in position like that might save a few vital seconds when the time came to make his escape. He would have to hope that Elizabeth Harper was the sort of young person who was able to shin down a rope when need arose.

A ladder led from the sentry walk down to the parade ground and Sykes slipped down this as quickly as he was able. From the sound of it there was a regular fiesta being celebrated in the makeshift shanty town outside the fort's gate. This should keep most of the people out of his way but, of course, there was always the possibility that the girl he had come for was also enjoying the party there.

It took Colonel Sykes a little while to get his bearings, but when he had done so he realized that he was not far from the office where Don Jose had interviewed him. Would his quarters be near by? And if so, would that be where Elizabeth Harper would be found? She was still free or at least had been a couple of hours ago when he had been spying on the fort.

There was no reason to suppose that a young girl would wish to stay in her room while everybody else was, by the sound of it, having such a good time. Did she even share Don Jose's quarters? Sykes had not given too much thought to the exact nature of their relationship, but had certainly assumed that she was the comanchero leader's lover or mistress. Who knew, with women?

Across the square he saw that one window had a light in it. For want of any better plan he thought that he would go and investigate this. Fortune was surely smiling upon the colonel that day, because not only did he see the girl he sought within the room, but she was also alone. He rapped softly upon the window pane.

Elizabeth Harper looked round startled, then gave a cry when she saw the colonel with his face pressed to the window. She came over and opened the casement, saying as she did so, 'Lord, you gave me a scare. Why are you prowling round like that? Anyway, you're supposed to be dead. I thought that the Comanches had sacrificed you.'

'It's by way of being a long story,' said Sykes. 'May I come in? We don't have much time.'

'Come in? You mean climb through my bedroom window? I never heard anything so scandalous in my life! What sort of reputation will I get with such goings on?'

'I shouldn't set too much store by your reputation as things now stand, Miss Harper, holed up with a bandit leader like this and him with a wife and all.'

'That's no affair of yours,' she said haughtily. 'Well, come in, if you're coming.'

The colonel clambered through the window and the girl closed it behind him.

'Have you no curtain we can draw?' he asked.

'This place does not run to curtains and soft furnishings, I am afraid. Anyway, what do you want?'

Colonel Sykes pulled out his watch and checked it. In considerably less than an hour Stanton would give the order to commence bombarding the fort with alternating rounds of canister and shot. They would have to move very swiftly.

He said, 'Miss Harper, your friend, Don Jose, is stringing you along, if you will forgive a vulgar expression. He has a wife and children in Mexico and has most definitely slept with some of the women you see round here. Those two men who took me off to the Comanche village are both illegitimate sons of his.'

The young woman did not speak at first, but then said quietly, 'You must think me a very fast piece of goods.'

Sykes smiled. 'It is not precisely the expression I should myself have chosen and your morals are no concern of mine. Will you come with me, right this very minute?'

'Of course,' said Elizabeth Harper, 'I had guessed some of this. Handsome man like that, well, it stands to reason he will have woman admiring him. Lovers even. But I thought I was special to him. What you just said, I know that's true. One of the half-breed girls here speaks a little English and she gave it me straight. She felt sorry for me. Imagine, being pitied by such a girl! How low I've sunk.' Then, to the colonel's absolute horror, the girl began sobbing in a quiet and hopeless way.

'Miss Harper,' Sykes said desperately, 'Elizabeth, we don't have time for all this. I'm not at all the proper person to hear your confessions. You need a priest or some such for that. My only aim is to get you out of here safely.'

'No, I must explain how it was, otherwise you will think me a right bad lot.'

It was on the tip of Colonel Sykes's tongue to tell the girl that he didn't much care if she *was* a bad lot, but he restrained himself. Always, always this sort of complication occurred whenever there was a woman in the case. Like as not, this wretched girl would now sit here crying and bemoaning her fate until the first shells from Captain Stanton's barrage landed on top of them.

He said, 'It really does not matter. I am not judging you.'

'Oh please, let me just tell you about Jose. My family come from Louisiana and I was a torment to them. Not at all how a respectable girl should be. My mother and father died of the typhoid fever and I was passed on to strangers, who packed me off to a school in Houston. In Texas, you know.'

'Yes,' said Sykes, exercising almost superhuman patience, 'I am familiar with the town.'

'Anyway, while I was there, I met Don Jose. I was only young. Well, it was over two years ago, so I guess I was eighteen. He was so charming and didn't take any liberties, if you know what I mean.'

Colonel Sykes shifted restlessly, wondering how quickly he could hurry this annoying young person through the recitation of her misfortunes. He was by no means a hard-hearted man, but had never had much patience with this sort of thing.

He said briskly, 'Anyway, all's well that ends well. Only be thankful that you found out in time the kind of man this Don Jose is. My, that's lucky. So if you are quite ready, we can leave now and I will take you to where you will be looked after well.'

The girl carried on as though she had not even heard him. 'We met regular for almost two months.

139

Which is a long time when you are that age.' The way
she talked, she might have been an old lady looking
back fifty or sixty years or more. 'I never thought to
see him again. I left school soon afterwards and then
stayed with some friends of my family who lived in
Texas. Then I was to go to California.'

Sykes did not ask why she had been going to
California. His sole aim was to hurry her along to the
end, so that they could make tracks. He glanced at
his watch again, but Elizabeth Harper seemed imper-
vious to hints of this sort.

'Miss Harper,' said Colonel Sykes, 'I fear that I
must speak bluntly, for which I hope that you will
forgive me and not take it amiss. If we do not leave
this very minute, we are apt to be caught up in some
pretty ferocious fighting. From all that I am able to
collect, most everybody is drinking, singing and so
on, over by the front gate. We are not likely to get a
better opportunity to escape.'

Maddeningly, the young woman forged on with
her narrative. There was something obsessive about
it, as though she would have no peace until she had
confessed all to him, a perfect stranger.

'The stage was jumped by Indians. I reckon you
know all about that. They took me prisoner and I
didn't know what would become of me. They didn't
speak English; leastways they wouldn't or couldn't
answer my questions. I was tied up and brought here.
Lord, I don't know what I thought was going to be
my fate. Then, like it was a fairy tale or something,
Jose appeared and turned out to be a man of great

consequence. Can you wonder that I fell into his arms? He was my protector. And so I . . . I gave myself to him.' She blushed crimson.

The colonel coughed and looked away. Then he said, 'It has come to the point, Miss Harper. Will you come with me now and escape from here?'

'It makes me feel kind of mean to Jose. I feel that I should bid him farewell for ever.'

'Don't even think of it,' said Sykes gruffly. 'He has it in mind to hold you hostage and demand a ransom for you from your uncle. I am sorry to have to tell you this, but you are little more to him than a marketable commodity.'

'How cruel and unfeeling you are!'

'Not a bit of it. I'm saving your life.'

'Very well. Let me gather up my things.'

'No, we leave right this very second. You will be climbing down a rope, I don't think you would want to be doing that carrying a suitcase.'

At last, to Colonel Sykes's immense relief, the girl agreed to leave Fort Bennett without further ado. He allowed her to gather up a few trifles such as a hair-brush and a daguerreotype of her mother. These she put in a clutch bag; then they were ready. According to Sykes's watch, it lacked only fifteen mintes to ten. They were cutting it a damned sight finer than he felt to be prudent.

'We had best not climb through the window,' said Sykes. 'I don't wish to attract any attention. Let us leave by the door and just walk, *walk* mind, don't run, to the ladder.'

Before they left the room Colonel Sykes extinguished the oil lamp and looked from the window. His heart sank. There was a cluster of men up on the rampart, right where he had climbed into the fort. He could hear them talking excitedly and it became apparent that they had discovered his rope and, for all he knew, the corpse of the fellow whose throat he had cut.

Without any clear idea of what he would do, Sykes led the woman to the door, which opened out on to the parade ground. He eased it open cautiously and when he was certain that nobody was near by, he urged the girl through it. The two of them scuttled along the side of the low building, keeping as far as possible out of the flickering light cast by the torches, which sputtered and flared above them.

There were other rough wooden ladders, built into the adobe and leading up to the sentry walk, which ran along the walls, but what point would there be in getting up there? It was perhaps a fifteen-foot drop to the ground, and even if *he* would risk the jump, the girl with him would probably end up at best with a sprained or even broken ankle. Sykes toyed with the notion of just walking out through the main gate and hoping that they could slip past the crowd of merrymakers.

It was too much of a risk. Perhaps he could try and shoot down the men blocking his way to the rope, which he had left dangling from the wooden beam? That too was a forlorn hope. The sound of gunfire would inevitably invite attention and the two of them

142

would probably not make it up the ladder, let alone over the wall.

Behind him, the girl was making various noises of the *What are we going to do?* type. Colonel Sykes led her round the corner of the building and found himself face to face with Don Jose, who was standing twenty feet away. At the same moment, as ill luck would have it, the men on the sentry walk also noticed him and the girl. They shouted a warning to Don Jose and two of them raised their rifles to cover Sykes.

'My dear Colonel,' said Don Jose smoothly, 'this is indeed an unexpected pleasure. I was quite sure that you would be dead by now, and yet here I find you roaming freely around my little domain. What a man you are!'

'Good evening, sir,' said Sykes. 'We seem fated to be at cross purposes. I dare say that my slinking along in the shadows like this looks a little suspicious to you?'

'You might say so, Colonel, you might say so. Elizabeth my dear, I am grieved to find that you have thrown in your lot with this person. It is not what I would have thought of you.'

'Oh, Jose. He said that you were going to sell me!'

'My dear, I thought we trusted each other. You would believe this wandering vagabond over me? Alas, that is cruel!'

'Don't listen to him, Miss Harper,' said Colonel Sykes irritably. 'You know as well as I do he's up to no good. He'd sell his own grandmother if there was sufficient profit to be made on the transaction.'

143

The Spaniard's face darkened, and for the first time, Sykes thought that his words had touched the man on the quick. He followed up this slight advantage by saying, 'He is a man without honour, a coward who dares not face his enemies on an equal footing. It runs in his blood. Those two curs whom he acknowledges as his sons are of the same brand. They only dared to attack me because I was tied up and helpless. Not one of those dogs would face a man in a fair fight.'

The colonel was pleased to see that Don Jose's face had become thunderous and his light, mocking air had wholly evaporated. He was breathing heavily. It was not perhaps a common experience for him to be derided and insulted after this fashion in his own lair. The men up on the wall had fallen silent, waiting to see what their chief would do and how he would dispose of this insolent stranger.

Don Jose said, 'Elizabeth, step away from the gentleman. He and I have a little business to conduct and I would not like to see you hurt in the process. As for you, my friend, you are a dead man.'

'Well, we shall see,' replied Colonel Sykes, a little taken aback that it had been so easy to goad the man into fighting like this, merely by impugning his honour. 'You're not the first person to make that threat. In fact, now I come to think of it, that's not the first time that you yourself have claimed that I was doomed. Yet here I am.'

'Yes, here you are. But not, I think, for much longer.'

Very slowly and carefully the Spaniard removed his white linen jacket and then, never once taking his eyes from the colonel, he walked over to a rail running along the side of the square and draped the jacket carefully over it. Then he made his way to the middle of the old parade ground and said to Sykes, 'Take your stand where you will, Colonel. You only have a few seconds of life remaining to you. Make the most of them.'

Colonel Sykes made his way to a spot on the parade ground about twenty yards from where Don Jose stood. The Spaniard's pistol hung from a fancy rig of tooled black leather and the flames of the torches reflected from what Sykes took to be some show-off, nickel-plated weapon.

'Carlo?' called Don Jose in Spanish. 'Snap your fingers for us a few times.'

The man who had escorted Colonel Sykes to Fort Bennett in the first place was evidently one of those up on the wall now. He snapped his fingers and the sound echoed across the square like a castanet.

'He has a rare talent,' said Don Jose. 'I have never met a man able to make a louder noise with his fingers.'

'What are you running here, Don Jose?' asked the colonel. 'A variety act? Why should you think that, at this point in my life, I would want to listen to one of your boys clicking his fingers?'

'It will be the last sound you ever hear. Carlo will give the signal. When he snaps his fingers, we fire. Is that a fair enough fight for you, Colonel?'

145

'I reckon so. But I could do with less chatter. Where I come from, men kill and are killed without making all this song and dance about the business.'

Trying to get Don Jose riled up was about the only way that Colonel Sykes could think of to give himself any kind of edge. His own fighting had not often run to duels like this and, all else being equal, he knew that he could not hope to compete with a man of this kind. He had succeeded in baiting and pushing Don Jose into this contest, but he knew that his chances of coming out of it alive were slender indeed.

'You are ready, then?' asked the Spaniard.

'I'm ready,' replied Sykes.

The two men faced each other in the gloom and, not for the first time in his life, Colonel Sykes figured that he might have come to the end of the road. He was proficient enough with pistols and could draw and fire as quickly as most men. For Don Jose, though, affairs like this were a full-time job.

There was nothing else in the world but the two of them, standing there on the old parade ground of Fort Bennett, about to find out which of them would live and who would die. In the distance Sykes could hear the sound of a guitar and a woman singing. There was rhythmic clapping as well and he could picture the scene as vividly as if he was present.

The woman's voice sounded a little melancholy and he wished that he might have seen her in the flesh. It was sad to think that his last sight in this life

146

was likely to be that suave bully eyeing him up at this very moment, like an undertaker measuring a corpse for his grave clothes.

Then two things happened, so close togther that they were all but simultaneous. Thinking back on it later, though, Colonel Sykes knew that this could not have been so and that he owed his very life to the fact that one of the events preceded the other, if only by the merest fraction of a second. How it seemed to him at that time, though, was that the man called Carlo had snapped his fingers and, at the same moment, Elizabeth Harper had cried out, 'Oh, Jose!' and run towards that gentleman across the square.

In reality, Elizabeth had shouted and begun to run just before the sound of Carlo's snapping fingers reached Colonel Sykes and the Spaniard. The comanchero leader had been distracted at the crucial moment and, although it caused him only the tiniest of delays, it was enough to cost him his life. Don Jose's pistol was out of the holster and almost levelled in his direction, when Colonel Sykes's ball took him in the chest. Sykes followed up almost immediately with a second shot to the head and the man fell dead.

Though he had killed his adversary, Sykes knew very well that the danger was not ended. He resisted the temptation to whirl and begin firing at the men looking down at him, several of them with rifles pointing in his direction. If he moved now it would be sufficient provocation for the men and they would shoot him down like a dog. Even so, his life was balanced on the edge of a knife. Then he heard, or thought he heard, one of the men above him, mutter, '*Adios!*' He tensed himself to receive the bullet.

CHAPTER 11

Colonel Sykes did not know whether or not he should say a prayer or take some evasive action. Neither course of action was likely to help at this late stage. He and the Lord had never been on very intimate terms, so he could scarcely expect the Deity to intervene on his behalf at this juncture. Moving, on the other hand, would be sure to pre-cipitate a hail of fire, so he simply stood stood, stock still, and awaited the inevitable. The crash of the explosion, when it came, was considerably louder than he had been anticipating. It sounded less like a shot from a rifle and more in the nature of an artillery shell.

The shower of debris which began to rain upon the parade ground caused the colonel to release his inhibitions about making any sudden movements. He turned to survey the wall, where a moment earlier six or seven men had been gazing down at him with evil intent. They had all been swept away by the round of canister shot that Captain Stanton had caused to be fired into the fort. Sykes took out his watch and checked the time. It was precisely ten; Stanton had been as good as his word.

Elizabeth Harper was crouched weeping over the bloody corpse of her one-time lover. Sykes swept his eyes over the point where he had climbed into Fort Bennett earlier that night. The explosion had caused only minor damage to the top of the wall, but had shattered the ladders leading up on to that section of the sentry walk. Lord knew where the rope was now: blown to atoms, most likely. As he stared at the carnage, the colonel became aware of the bodies and parts of bodies of those who had been menacing him. They were scattered over a pretty wide area and could be left out of the reckoning in his future plans, which was a mercy.

The singing and guitar-playing had, not unnaturally, stopped and been replaced by the angry shouts of men and the terrified screaming of women. That Stanton must be a cold-blooded bastard, thought Sykes, to open fire with artillery like that on a party of men and women who were doing nothing more than having a party. He knew that he himself could never have given such an order to a gun crew. If this was the new kind of warfare he wanted no part of it. Where was the honour or glory in such an action?

There came a concussion strong enough to shake the ground beneath his feet and more cries of fear and distress. Stanton's howitzer was getting the range now and would, Sykes supposed, be pounding this place systematically to pieces. If he did not get the girl out of there directly all his efforts would have been in vain. He went over to where Elizabeth was sobbing.

'Miss Harper,' he said, 'If we stay here, then you are apt to share the fate of that devil lying there in the dust. Come!'

The young woman turned a white face up to him.

'You killed him,' she said wonderingly. 'Just shot him down without any hesitation. What sort of man are you?'

'A man with a job to do,' said Sykes, grabbing her by the arm and yanking her to her feet. 'Come on.'

The girl suffered herself to be hustled across the square towards a section of the wall where the ladders were still intact. There was another explosion, which demolished half of a barrack block on the other side of the compound. The girl clutched at Colonel Sykes in fear.

'What will become of us?'

'Don't fear, Miss Harper. We are not finished yet.'

Sykes's mind was working furiously. There was no point in trying to get out of the fort through the main gate. If the comancheros didn't shoot them they would be blown to pieces by one of Stanton's shells. It was unlikely that the girl could be persuaded to jump fifteen feet from the top of one of those walls either. Should they just shelter here and hope for the best? That too seemed a poor choice.

It had been Stanton's plan to reduce the fort to

rubble by use of his artillery piece. Odds were that he and the girl would die if they didn't get out of Fort Bennett by one means or another, and that pretty soon.

It was then that he remembered the barrel of gunpowder, which he was still carrying slung round his neck on a piece of rope. How could he have been so stupid?

There was another boom, this one even closer than the last.

Sykes said, 'Just set right here, Miss Harper. Don't move a muscle, you hear me? I'm sorry to speak so, but it is life and death now.'

Then, from the front of the fort, Colonel Sykes heard a sound that chilled his blood. It was the unmistakable, staccato hammering of a Gatling gun. The good Lord alone knew what Stanton's reaction would be to that. One thing was certain sure: this place would soon be a free-fire zone, with anybody or anything which moved becoming the target of one side or the other.

Leaving the girl standing in the shadow of the nearest building, Sykes sprinted over to the wall and examined it. As he had thought, it was basically nothing more substantial than sun-baked mud reinforced by wooden stakes. He hacked frantically away at the base of the wall with the Indian knife. It was a pity to use such a fine implement for coarse work, but needs must when the devil drove.

When he had excavated a cavity a little larger in size than his powder keg he inserted the wooden barrel into the hole and opened the bung. Into this he inserted the fuse. Twenty feet was too long, so he sawed off about a third of that length and then pushed that into the barrel.

There was more shooting from the gate, rifle fire by the sound of it, interspersed with bursts from a Gatling. Then there was another terrific explosion. Sykes took a box of lucifers from his pocket and lit the fuse. He ran back to where Elizabeth Harper was waiting and dragged her round the corner of the building.

They were only just in time because, with a mighty roar, a forty-foot section of the rear wall of the fort was blown to smithereens by his mine. When he peeped round the corner the devastation that his five pounds of powder had wrought was wonderful to behold. The most important point was that there was now nothing to hinder him and the girl from escaping at once.

It was impossible to work out what was happening in and around Fort Bennett. Sykes did not know whether the comancheros were actually engaging Stanton's troopers in battle or were just shooting into the darkness. At a guess, they could see the flashes when the howitzer fired and were directing their fire towards it. If he had been Captain Stanton, he would not have hazarded his men until he was quite sure all resistance was crushed in here.

'We must make a bolt for it,' he told the frightened girl. 'Do you understand? You must run as fast as you are able. I don't want anybody to be able to draw a bead on us. It is the home run now, Miss Harper.'

It was, he thought, the hell of a thing for a young person like this to have to go through. For his part, he was exhilarated by the gunfire and explosions, but from all that he could collect the girl at his side was terrified out of her wits by it all. The pine torches were no longer providing the only light in the fort. Away over towards the gate a building had caught fire and Sykes had the impression that other fires were starting as well.

He took the girl's hand and said, 'Right, run for your very life!'

The two of them raced to the gap in the wall and then they were out of the fort. It was pitch black here; the sky was overcast and the moon was obscured by clouds. Colonel Sykes only hoped that he was able to lead them in a straight line. It wouldn't do for them to start wandering in circles in the dark. There was not really much fear of that, because the beleagured fort was like a beacon in the night. All they had to do was keep their backs to the flames and they could be reasonably sure of striking the dried-up riverbed.

The girl had said nothing since Don Jose had died and Colonel Sykes was feeling a mite uneasy about her.

He said, 'You all right there, miss? You're not going to have the hysterics or anything, are you?'

'You and Jose are much the same as each other, you know. That's what he said after you went off the other day. He said you were both cut from the same piece of cloth.'

This was a disturbing thought and the colonel didn't much care for it. He said roughly, 'Well, I guess you have had a better deal from me than you ever did from him, at any rate.'

'Have I?' she said. 'He was exciting and fun to be with; you're like a man fetching an order of groceries from the store. I'd a sight sooner spend time with Jose than I would with you.'

Colonel Sykes considered inviting the girl to return to the fort if that was how she felt about it, but then decided that such a statement would be unworthy of him. He limited himself to saying, 'Well, I did what I thought was right and I reckon that's all any of us can do.'

Once they reached the riverbed the two of them climbed gingerly down, slithering the last few feet. The moon emerged from the clouds, shedding its pallid light over the stony watercourse. The mare that Sykes had borrowed from Camp Edgewood was revealed to be standing perhaps fifty yards away, not at all troubled by the gunfire and explosions, which were now increasing in frequency.

'We're likely to be here for some few hours,' said the colonel. 'I will grant that it is not the most comfortable spot, but you might wish to try and get a little sleep.'

'Sleep? After seeing somebody murdered in front of my eyes? It's likely, isn't it!'

And this, thought Colonel Sykes, is a specimen of the thanks one receives for saving a person from a bandit stronghold and having your life saved into the bargain. Never again would he concern himself in any project which had at its heart a woman!

CHAPTER 12

Sykes and the girl did not exchange another word that night. The two of them sat, side by side, in the darkness, listening to the destruction of Fort Bennett and the killing of those who had lately been living there. As the night drew on the explosions and gunfire became less frequent until they died out altogether. The colonel risked lighting a lucifer and checking his watch. It was three in the morning. He looked at Elizabeth Harper, whose eyes were closed, although he was sure that she was not sleeping.

Although cowering like this in the stony riverbed was uncomfortable, Sykes was damned if he was going to jump up in the darkness and announce his presence to the army. If he knew anything about how such operations were conducted they would even now be scouring the country for survivors of their massacre. They would be shooting first, as well, then only later finding that they had shot a woman or other non-combatant.

When dawn came Sykes said to the girl, 'Come, it

should be safe enough now to declare our presence. I need to hand you over to somebody.' Even as the words left his mouth he regretted them; he sounded like somebody talking of delivering a parcel. What was it she had said last night, that he acted like a man collecting groceries from a store? Well, he was a soldier. What did she expect?

The fort had been reduced to a heap of ruins. Stanton's troopers were busy establishing their camp near by and the colonel saw that the Gatling guns had been secured. Captain Stanton was surprised, but pleased to see them.

'Colonel Sykes, Miss Harper,' he said. 'I guessed that you would be keeping out of range until we had finished our little job. We will be spending a couple of days here, but then we can all travel back to Edgewood together.'

'I am sure that Miss Harper will be glad of that. For my part, I am going in quite another direction,' said the colonel. 'But thank you for the offer.'

'Where are you going?' asked Stanton.

'South.'

'You're really going to join Juàrez, then? I would have thought you had seen enough action lately to last you for a good long time.'

Colonel Sykes said nothing for a spell, then he remarked, 'I don't much care for the wars that you and those like you are now waging. Shelling civilians, Gatling guns; the whole lot of it. Maybe Juàrez and the Mexicans are still fighting in a cleaner way.'

'I wouldn't bank on it,' said Captain Stanton

sourly. 'Not from what I have heard of the business.'

'Whether or no, I am done here. There is a trunk of my clothes at Camp Edgewood. It would be nice to think that they will find their way back to Milledgeville. As for the horse and guns I borrowed, well, I reckon that I will hang on to them for the time being.'

'You earned them, Colonel. I don't think anybody else could have freed Miss Harper here. I will square that with Major Sterne.'

Sykes turned to Elizabeth Harper and said, 'I'm sorry about killing your friend, Miss Harper. I was only doing what I felt I should, but still and all, I am sorry.'

The girl shrugged. 'I guess it don't signify now. I know you saved my life, for which I thank you.'

There being nothing else to say, the colonel shook hands with Captain Stanton and made his way back to where the mare was waiting for him. Stanton and the girl watched as he walked back to the river. Then he dropped over the bank and was lost to sight.

Home Library Service (For Staff Use Only)

1	2	3	4	5	6	7	8	9
		326A						

27094